The Bachelor on
MARS

LEIGH WYNDFIELD

OMNI*fic*
PUBLISHING
LOS ANGELES

Omnific Publishing
2355 Westwood Blvd., Suite 506
Los Angeles, CA 90064
www.omnificpublishing.com

First Omnific eBook edition, September 2021
First Omnific trade paperback edition, September 2021

Library of Congress Cataloguing-in-Publication Data

Wyndfield, Leigh.
The Bachelor on Mars / Leigh Wyndfield – 1st ed. ISBN: 978-1-623422-70-7
1. Contemporary Romance — Fiction. 2. Mars — Fiction.
3. Science — Fiction. 4. Humor — Fiction. I. Title

10 9 8 7 6 5 4 3 2 1

Cover Design by Sweet n' Spicy Designs
Interior Book Design by Amit Dey
Printed in the United States of America

CHAPTER ONE

*M*argaret Carson rose from a crouch, wrench in hand, to find her research assistant Taylor fidgeting on the far side of the lift. The graduate students always seemed to be fidgeting, as if she made them nervous, which was silly. She wasn't an ogre, just no-nonsense and direct.

"Yes?" she asked, hoping the interruption would be fast. If she adjusted the drive shaft a tiny bit, she knew the rover she'd spent the last five years working on would be perfect.

"Dr. Carson, I know you asked not to be disturbed."

"True." She couldn't return to work until she dealt with whatever Taylor had to tell her, so Margaret forced herself to focus.

"A man is here who says he's your brother," Taylor said in a rush, her voice breathy and higher than usual, her face shining with fascination. "I didn't even know you *had* a brother."

Every woman had this reaction to Hank. Her whole family had been blessed in the good-looks department, a trait that had been a hindrance more than once in her career. As a mechanical engineer, her appearance should never be more important than her brain, so she'd learned to be as incognito as possible. She accomplished this by wearing what she called her uniform— black pants, a shapeless golf shirt and no makeup. Her hair was always in an unsophisticated ponytail and she'd added glasses despite not needing them. She suspected she'd taken the slightly sloppy look too far, but it was so comfortable, she'd be okay if she never wore high heels again.

"Show him in," she said with a sigh. If her brother had come in person, then the four messages he'd left earlier really *had* been important after all, which wasn't necessarily true when it came to her brother.

She'd planned to call him in a couple hours. *After* she'd finished the adjustment she'd woken up in the middle of the night knowing would solve the drive train problem that had cropped up last week on the rough terrain simulating Mars. Which was where her rover would ultimately end up, when she won the grants to pay to test it on the red planet.

Margaret stared fondly at her creation, the domed passenger compartment that could carry two people sitting atop supports that went down to eight wheels like a gigantic, bad ass spider. The struts could flex and bend to accommodate obstacles and uneven ground. The odd wheel base allowed it to climb, solving the current issue with normal rovers getting trapped by sudden breaks in the terrain. The compartment would keep two people in a perfectly controlled oxygen environment. In the rear, two solar panels flared like wings.

The unmanned rovers of the past had run into issues with solar, because the panels had been quickly covered by the dust that swirled in the Mars wind. They had replaced their solar with nuclear, which had a lifespan of only two years. But her rovers carried people, who could easily wipe off the dust, giving them a never-ending power supply that should be perfect.

Maybe if she added another shock absorber up at the top of each wheel strut, she'd be able to lessen the abuse to the drive train. She leaned down to study the top of the struts.

"Margo," her brother said from somewhere above her, making her jump because she'd already forgotten him.

"Hank," she said, straightening, blinking a bit to bring him into focus.

Her brother's name was Harold, but he was not a Harold. Her brother was the least stuffy, most fun-loving guy she knew. Women and even men flocked to him, with his blond hair and easy smile, straight teeth, glowing green eyes, and perfect body. Today he was dressed as a TV executive, which was what he did for a living.

Her brother frowned in concern, clearly wondering as all her family did, how this had happened. This being her whole mechanical engineering fixation and her lack of personal style. "I have a proposition for you."

She didn't have time for one of her brother's schemes, so she said, "No," and leaned over to the rover.

Hank knocked on the rover's hood.

She stumbled backwards in surprise, having already drifted into work. "Why are you still here? You know I don't participate in your crazy plans anymore, *Harold*."

"I know you don't usually, *Margaret*," he said, stressing her full name as she had stressed his, but the difference was, she liked it better when he called her by her name. She was the one person in the family who appreciated a stuffy handle. "But this time, you will be glad you listened to me."

Margaret straightened and put on her patience hat. The way to get rid of Hank was to hear it all the way through and then be firm and clear. When her brother dug in like this, he wasn't going to go away without fully exploring his skills of persuasion. While tenacity was one of her own positive attributes, she found it annoying in others. "I'm listening."

"You know my latest TV show?"

She strained her brain, but the file folder came up empty. "No." She loved her brother and knew he loved her, but they were completely opposite people, and as such had a hard time finding each other interesting.

Hank threw up his hands, clearly exasperated. "Margo, do you ever notice what anyone else does with their lives?"

"Not really," she admitted, wondering why he looked so huffy. She wished no one ill, she just had better things to do with her time. She glanced at the rover. Like work.

Hank knocked on the rover's hood again, annoying her. "Don't ignore me when I've driven all the way over here to talk to you."

She stepped away from her work, because she wouldn't be able to stand near and not focus on it. "Then talk."

"My latest show I'm producing is called The Mars Bachelor."

"Oh, good lord," she whispered, but softly, because she couldn't get rid of him without him saying whatever it was he'd come to say.

"It takes place on Mars, of course."

She blinked. "But that would cost millions."

Hank huffed out a laugh. "You have no idea. We can't film without two rockets to move both the people and equipment up and back down, which would blow your mind it's so expensive. Then we have to pay to live in some crappy research station that is about one step up from camping despite a daily rate that is triple the Ritz per person."

The full impact hit her. "Wait! Are you telling me you'll get to Mars before I will, Hank? Because if you're telling me that, we both know that's completely unfair." She'd spent her life trying to get to the red planet.

"Have you ever watched *The Bachelor*?" he asked, ignoring her question.

"Of course not," she said, insulted.

"My God, it's like you're not even part of our generation," he said, shaking his head. "Okay, so the premise is that women compete to end up engaged to one man. He slowly weeds them out until he's left with The One." He made air quotes around the last two words.

She hissed. "That is one of the most hideous, misogynistic things I've ever heard, and you're *producing it*?"

"Settle down," he said, grinning at her, not insulted in the least by her criticism. He never was. "They have the same show in reverse where the woman picks from a group of men."

"Still disgusting, even if the woman is picking," she informed him, but had to secretly admit it wasn't as gross.

"Disgusting or not, we have plenty of money to go to any place our viewers can dream up. We're set to leave tomorrow for Mars."

She moaned in jealousy. Her brother, who had once declared that only geeks were interested in space, was going on her dream trip.

Going to Mars would be commonplace in the next twenty or thirty years, now that they'd solved the space travel puzzle. With the introduction of new rockets and a cheap fuel source, it was only a three-week trip instead of three hundred days. But for today, only scientists and a small few were given visas to go up and even then, the price was astronomical.

But somehow her brother and a group of desperate-to-be-in-love women were heading up to the red planet before she was. She gripped a nearby lab table to steady herself.

Hank raised his fist as if to knock on her rover again.

"You better not," she warned, but she wasn't really angry. It was impossible to stay mad at Hank since he was in a continuous good mood. And it wasn't his fault he was going to Mars before her. He'd probably done market research and found Mars was the number one filming location for high ratings. And she had to admit, even she would be tempted to watch.

He laughed and lowered his hand. "One of the contestants fell and broke her leg last night. We need a fill in." He looked at Margaret expectantly.

She made a hurry up motion with one hand, wondering why he'd paused. Surely he'd be gone soon, so she could get back to work.

He shook his head, wearing a look that he often had when they talked. "You." He pointed at her. "I need *you* to fill in."

"You want me to be on a show where a man picks through women like he would choose a dog at the pound?"

He nodded. "*On Mars.*"

Mars.

Oh, God. Would she give up her pride to go to Mars? "Why me?" she asked. He had other people to choose from, like someone who wanted to put themselves in a debasing and probably humiliating position.

"Who else would I think of? You've talked about little else since we were kids. And very few people are sitting around with all the psych evaluations, medical tests, physical conditioning requirements, and vaccines completed." Hank gave her an assessing look. "Besides, you're beautiful and I need a gorgeous woman. And we can play up the brainy professor thing."

"Great. Just what I've always longed for. The opportunity to be valued for my looks." Another thought occurred to her. "Wait a minute, you think I'll let you publicly humiliate me in front of all my peers on a national TV show?"

Hank nodded. "International. The show is in every English speaking country and dubbed in three languages." Hank's pride at this fact was clear.

"You're insane," she whispered, staring at her brother with wonder. Did he have no idea who she was? She would never risk her reputation like this, even if Mars was her biggest dream. "I have spent my life building my academic reputation. I would never live it down if I went on your show."

"This show is not about humiliating women, Margo." His tone turned annoyed. "It's about love."

"Love is for saps and losers, Hank."

"How is it possible you and I are from the same family?" he asked, his voice filled with awe, because Hank was a man who loved deeply and often.

"No one was ever remembered throughout history for being *in love*," she said, trying to explain. Her life was about making this world better, creating solutions to hard problems. She wanted to leave her stamp on science long after she was gone.

"How about Romeo and Juliet?"

She covered her eyes with her hands. Did her brother not read? "They were fourteen-year-olds who killed themselves. Besides, they weren't even real people. Shakespeare made them up."

Hank stared at her with that determined look on his face. The same one that had once had him heckling her until she'd been the lead in a play he'd written, a memory that still made her burn with humiliation every time she thought of it. He pointed at the rover. "If you come fill in, I promise to give you a fake name, hide your identity, and—"

She opened her mouth to cut him off.

He raised his voice to finish, "—you can test your rover."

She closed her mouth, staring at him in shock. Test her rover. On Mars.

He knew he had her hooked, because he held up one finger. "You get to test it *after* you're voted off the show. Not before."

Reality hit her. "I have a budget meeting I can't miss in two months." Even with the decreased time to get to Mars and back, there was no way she would make it. And if she wasn't there, her lab funding would be the first on the chopping block.

"We've got two rockets scheduled. One with the original cast and a second coming less than a week later that will bring new supplies and take those home who are voted out in the first few rounds. It's the regular quarterly supply run for the station. Boyle made us pay for it." Hank made a sour face. "You would come back just in time to make your meeting, although expect to be badly space lagged."

She started to say no again, but asked instead, "I'll get voted off at the beginning?" All her pride fell away like her weight loss resolutions in the face of chocolate. Test her rover. And Hank promised she'd be anonymous. She'd slap on makeup and dye her hair. Take off her glasses.

"Right. You'll go first for sure. With your acting skills, we'll have to edit you out as it is." He looked grumpy at the thought. "You're going to end up being a bigger pain in the ass than dealing with Jack Boyle."

"Jack Boyle, the geologist?" she asked, drawn up short by the famous name.

Hank nodded. "He runs the station."

"Jack Boyle is letting a reality TV show film at Research Station 7?" Holy smokes. His reputation made him sound like he'd never sell out. She'd seen him speak a few times. He had a hot mind and a pretty decent body. He was, in fact, her definition of perfection in the male species.

"You know the number of his research station?" her brother asked, acting like she knew the name of an obscure last century rock band.

"Hank, there are only two active stations on Mars right now. It's not exactly hard to keep up with two numbers. Besides, Jack Boyle is a super star."

"Jack Boyle is a grumpy, hard-headed asshole."

A horrible thought occurred to her. "He isn't the bachelor is he?"

Hank laughed for so long, she figured the answer was no.

"It's not *that* unlikely. He's pretty hot for a geologist." When she'd seen him at a Mars Exploration event last year, he'd actually handed her some papers she'd dropped and she'd checked him out up close. Definitely a ten in her book.

Her brother swiped at tears, annoying her further.

She decided to ignore his mirth, since he obviously thought her personal idea of a perfect mate wasn't bachelor worthy. Hank never could appreciate science. "Wow, Jack Boyle, I've always wanted to meet him." But oh no! She'd meet him as a contestant on an embarrassing TV show. She'd have to duck him if at all possible. "How will I be anonymous?" she asked, seeing complications everywhere.

But Boyle didn't know who she was. Besides, he barely spoke to anyone. He might have published the most far-reaching studies on rock formations on Mars, but he was basically a recluse, totally focused on his research.

Hank scanned her up and down appraisingly. "Because we'll turn you into the knockout you are, hiding under all that."

She stared at her lab coat and tennis shoes. "I work in a lab. This is practical attire." Besides, this was her uniform, not rags.

"Just trust me. Our own mother won't recognize you after my people get done."

This is a bad idea. It will all go wrong, her mind warned. *No one keeps secrets anymore.*

She looked at her rover. Mars. She'd finally get to Mars and test her rover. No more late night grant work, no more begging for funding. She'd be there.

"Two days work max and you can spend the time until the next shuttle testing. You'll have at least a couple days of experiments, before the second shuttle arrives." Hank gave her his here-is-your-biggest-wish smile. "This might be your only chance in the next ten years and I'm handing it to you on a silver platter."

"This is going to be a disaster," she whispered, but she was going and he knew it.

"Great! It's settled then," Hank said. "You need to be packed and at this address before six tonight. I've got a crew in route here to pick up the rover and whatever else you need for your tests." He put a stack of papers on a nearby workbench, "You can't get on the shuttle without signing these liability forms. The company won't be responsible if anything goes wrong. You're going to another planet—"

She cut him off. "I know where I'm going. Probably better than you do."

He grinned, happy and easygoing now that he'd gotten his way. "You do. So, I'll see you tonight, sis." He leaned over and planted a big, loud kiss on her cheek. "You won't regret this," he said, as he jaunted to the door.

"Wait! What do you get out of all this?" she called, suddenly suspicious. Because she'd just received her biggest dream.

"An Emmy," he said and disappeared.

Watching him go, excitement warred with nerves, making her stomach ache.

But her heart wasn't going to let her pass on the opportunity to go to Mars.

"Taylor," she called to her assistant.

"Yes?" Taylor came out of a nearby office as if she'd been waiting to catch another look at Hank. Which she probably had been.

"How would you like to run this lab while I take care of a family emergency?" Margaret asked, knowing she was giving Taylor a huge increase in stature by putting her in charge of the lab.

Taylor's eyes grew huge. "You, you want me to run the lab?"

Margaret nodded, pleased she'd followed her instincts. Taylor would work her ass off to make sure everything went smoothly. "I've been watching you and you're ready."

"I am?" the young woman asked. "I mean, *I am*." She nodded, obviously trying to cover her shock.

Margaret wasn't into the women solidarity thing that some of her colleagues were, but the fact was, women *did* have a harder time getting ahead in mechanical engineering, a field dominated by men. "Go get a notebook and take down a list of what you need to do."

Margaret looked at her rover. Maybe this would turn out to be a horrible idea, but she was going to Mars, dammit. "I'm going to get everything I've ever wanted," she whispered, and for the first time in as long as she could remember, she smiled.

CHAPTER TWO

*A*few hours later, Margaret ignored the instructions to wait in the green room and instead wandered around the loading zone until she'd located her rover. She felt almost compelled to be there when it was loaded, feeling like a mother about to see her child off to school for the first time. Working with the foreman, she personally wielded the drill to box the vehicle, making sure it was protected from any jostling during their launch.

"Here you are," Hank said behind her, making her jump and the last screw go sideways. "Margo, we don't have time for this. Everyone is on the rocket but you."

"I'm not going all the way to Mars to find my rover in pieces when we arrive." She hurriedly screwed the last board in place, not wanting to be left behind, although they hadn't even started the precheck yet.

Hank let out a huff of exasperation. "You know, there are other people on Earth who can do just as good a job as you at something like this."

She doubted it, but allowed him to pull the drill from her hand and haul her back into the building. This trip to Mars meant everything to her, but she would only be on the planet for a very short time. She needed to be ready to spring into action and start testing. The last thing she needed was to arrive on Mars and find her rover needed major repairs.

"Here she is," he said, handing her off to a woman with a clipboard.

"Let's get you onboard," the woman said, already walking away with brisk efficiency.

"Hank," Margaret said, stopping her brother when he turned to go back down the ramp. "Thank you. Really. This means the world to me." While her brother drove her crazy, she knew she owed him for getting her and her rover to Mars.

"I know," Hank said, and grinned at her. "I'll see you soon."

"Aren't you coming?"

"To fit your rover, we needed to cut some weight. I'll be there three days after you."

"Wait, what?" she asked, but the efficient woman had come back and herded her along with a shooing motion, a little more enthusiastically than necessary in Margaret's opinion.

Hank waved, an annoying grin on his face, as if he'd played a great joke on her.

Margaret hoped she was imagining things. Before she could decide, they were on the rocket, the woman stuffing Margaret into a seat and handing her a helmet, then disappearing as quickly as she'd come.

Eleven women surrounded her, everyone already strapped in, so Margaret strapped in too. She was surrounded by the most gorgeous group of people she'd ever seen in one room before. It was hard not to stare.

Luckily, she was distracted by an official voice over the intercom. "Please prepare for takeoff."

And then it hit her like a ton of bricks. She was going to *Mars*. It was her dream come true. She was doing it. She'd worry about her brother and the TV show when she arrived. For now, she would hold this moment close and cherish it.

The room they'd been assigned on the rocket was round, of course. She'd watched a PBS special on the building of it, so she knew the architect had decided to put in a round sofa circling the space, with navy blue cushions. Each section folded out as a bed for a contestant, then converted to a daytime sofa, then converted into a jump seat for takeoff and landing.

"Helmets on please ladies," came a bouncy voice over a loud speaker.

A groan filled the cabin. "My hair," someone near her whined.

"Helmet hair," another agreed. "I hope they let us wash it when we get there."

"Won't happen," a third woman said in a know-it-all tone. "No water, remember? They had a whole section on that in the manual."

Margaret put hers on without a thought. Her hair was always a mess. Besides, if she had to dress in a clown suit to get to Mars, she would. In fact, if she thought about it, she had basically joined a circus to get on the red planet.

And suddenly the whole rocket began to shake. Vaguely she could hear a countdown, but then the rumble built to a rage and the whole ship shook with the force building under it as the blasters fired.

Then something released them and they were flung into the air, pinning her into her seat, gravity bearing down on her at an incredible force. Around her, women screamed and moaned, but Margaret couldn't stop grinning. This. Was. Awesome.

It took hours, but they were finally released from their seats and the heat shielding was retracted to reveal a large viewport to the stars. Everyone gathered around, fighting their way to the window and for a moment, every contestant was as awed as Margaret. But within a few minutes, they grew bored of the never-ending stars and the women drifted away, the excitement fading. Soon everyone returned to lounge on their sofas, leaving Margaret alone.

I'm going to Mars. It's going to be amazing.

She planned to suck the marrow out of every second of every minute of every one of the hours she'd be on this journey, as well as the time she'd spend on the planet. This trip was going to change her life. She was sure of it. Once she stood on Mars, a seed inside her was going to germinate and grow, and from that new born plant, her career would blossom to the next level, allowing her to become the scientist she'd always known she could be. The grant money would come to her. No more begging for funds and selling her concepts to NASA.

She wished she had someone who understood to share this moment with, but no one, not even her brother, could understand.

Although without her brother, she would have never had this chance. Hank might be a pain in the ass at times, but he'd gotten her on this rocket, so she owed him big.

"I don't think my hair will ever be the same after wearing that helmet," one of the women said behind her.

Then again, her brother had come up with an idea of sending a bunch of women to Mars who were more concerned with their hair than going to another planet.

Tuning them all out, Margaret promised not to let anything kill her buzz. The excitement and euphoria swirled around her, so effervescent, it raised gooseflesh on her arms.

Staring at an ocean of stars before her, Margaret realized she'd been waiting for this moment since she was ten years old. And it was finally here.

Jack Boyle drove his rover to the small valley he'd been exploring, taking a quick trip before he was locked in Station 7's biodome for the next month. He'd discovered some unusual basalt samples and wanted to grab more before the TV people descended upon him like locusts. Parking close to the site, he sealed his suit, eager to enjoy the few hours he'd have to work before his "guests" arrived and filming began.

As he ran through his safety checklist, he tried to stop dwelling on the coming weeks of utter and complete hell he'd have to endure, all because he and Station 7 needed the money. Desperately.

Everything cost so much, no matter how he'd tried to cut corners and he'd been on the verge of doing something drastic, maybe even shutting down the station. When he'd been contacted by Hank Carson about hosting the show at Station 7, he'd known that no matter how unpleasant it might be, he would tolerate twelve reality TV show contestants and two producers moving in with him for the duration just so he could keep the station running for another year.

"Oh, and don't forget the bachelor," he growled out loud, so disgusted he couldn't keep quiet.

A reality TV show where women vied to be chosen by a bachelor. Jack admitted it appealed to him on a primal level. His twenty-year-old self might have wanted to be the bachelor. Now his thirty-five-year-old self thought the whole thing was an annoying waste of his time.

But he had no choice.

When Jack first opened Research Station 7, he'd been euphoric. There was something to be said about accomplishing his life's work before most were hitting the prime of their careers. But then reality had come crashing in on him. Running a station had turned out to be paperwork and pain. He'd built this station to run experiments, but he barely had time to run them. The fact was, he'd never been good at money. He was best in the field, doing what God had intended him to do, which was look at rocks.

This morning he'd gather as many samples as he could to study while he was locked in the station riding herd on the TV people. A small little bone he'd decided to throw himself.

As he walked to the top of a volcanic rift that spread across the surface, he said the mantra he'd developed to help him through the next four weeks, "I will be nice to the TV people. I will not yell at them or toss them out of the biodome. They are keeping Station 7 alive and therefore I must be nice." Even if he didn't want to be nice. Even if he wanted to send old Hank a message and tell him to go find another location for his show.

"I will be nice," he said again, for good measure. Because the fact was, he wasn't nice. The best anyone could say was that he was direct in his communication style. It really hadn't mattered that much. After all, rocks didn't complain.

He forgot about the incoming rabble as he took in the view.

Mars was desolate and windswept, but utterly beautiful. Below him, a craggy valley of basalt, shale, and sandstone stretched out for miles in either direction, the valley floor a set of plates that had shifted and broken into what he thought of as massive tiles of the gods. The far valley wall rose up in a mound of sand, a massive dune several football fields long looking like a perfectly smooth surface from here, but he knew under it all would most likely be another set of rocks, trapping the sand there.

He opened his kit and began collecting samples.

When the alarm buzzer sounded that the TV people would be landing in two hours, it startled him. He was always surprised by how quickly time flew when he was working. With a sad heart, he put away all his supplies in a duffle and picked it up.

He'd drifted further away from the rover than he'd realized. Picking up speed, he bounded west. Since Mars had less mass than Earth, he weighed less and therefore had to walk or run in an odd, convoluted gate. It was more of a push off and glide motion.

He'd only taken four leaps when a tremendous crack rang out, the soil beneath his feet shifting and churning as if a small earthquake had shivered past him.

He stopped his forward momentum by jumping up instead of out, skidding to a stop.

At first, he thought a fault had shifted but then he realized the sound had come from the direction of his rover.

Instinctively, Jack hunkered down behind a large bolder. Nothing was alive bigger than a bacterium on Mars. There were no giant sandworms or human-sized, flesh-eating bats. But he'd sensed the tremor. Something was out there.

He waited ten minutes, but it remained quiet.

Time passed and he felt foolish. He should go over and see if the rover was still in one piece. There was nothing to worry about, since there was no one on this entire planet but the people at Station 5 and him. At least not for the next couple hours.

Placing his hand on a rock to stand, a motion caught his eye. A matte black craft rose up from where his rover had been parked. Small and egg shaped, it slowly made its way to the north, flying only a few feet above the surface.

Jack ducked down again out of sight.

The ship was like nothing he'd ever seen and at first his mind screamed *aliens*, but then his common sense took over and he realized it must have been from Russia or maybe even China.

Both countries had been threatening to come to Mars for years, ever since he and Walter Haxley had opened their stations. They didn't want to get too far behind in the space race.

After studying the sky and finding it clear, Jack carefully worked his way to his rover.

For a moment, his brain struggled to take in the smoking pile of rubble that had been his only remaining conveyance.

He was well and truly screwed. His pack list had included two rovers when he moved here, but he'd run out of money long before the first vehicle needed expensive repairs.

Looked like he'd be walking back. He was in deep shit, and he knew it. He blew out a breath to calm his thumping heart and bottle up the fear.

Glancing at the small screen on his wrist, he checked his oxygen level. Only six hours left. Could he make it back to the station on that? He glanced at the sun and realized he barely had enough time to return before dark. He would never survive out here at night with the temperatures plummeting sometimes below -70 degrees Celsius.

The TV people would be landing soon, but luckily he'd programmed a robot to haul their ship into the biodome without him being there. Trying to figure out where fifteen extra people would sleep had been the hardest part of the negotiations, but it had been simple enough to bring the rocket into the courtyard and use it as a temporary hotel.

The biodome had revolutionized living on Mars, making it habitable for people to spend long periods of time here. It was a transparent shield that allowed sunlight in, while keeping out storms and the most extreme temperatures changes. It maintained an atmosphere close to Earth's, which reduced the wear and tear space living did to the human body. The rocket couldn't use the small door Jack had for the rover to move in and out, so he'd had to program the biodome to temporarily peel back for the time it took to enter. Carson's people would have to use a canvas walkway between their ship and his lab to protect the contestants until the atmosphere returned to normal. Jack would just have to hope everything went smoothly until he returned.

If he returned.

He calmed his breathing. Every sip of air was one closer to the end of his reserve. It would be a balancing act to make it back without suffocating. If he went too fast, he'd use his oxygen up quickly. If he went too slow, he'd simply run out of air before he reached his destination.

The important thing now was not to panic. It was imperative he get home alive so he could send the TV people right back to Earth before the Chinese or the Russians attacked Station 7.

<hr />

They landed five hours early, well before dark. As the robot pulled them into the biodome, Margaret watched from a window, taking in every sight she could. Craggy mountains loomed in the far distance, a purplish red in the haze. The ground was red and dusty and barren. She shivered with anticipation. This was it. This was the moment she'd waited for her whole life.

Behind her, the women got to know each other, chatting about their lives and making guesses about who the bachelor would be. She let their words wash over her, realizing they were as excited about the bachelor as she was about getting to Mars.

It wouldn't have mattered to them if they were going to Aruba or Cancun or Pluto. The destination didn't matter. To them, Mars was just a means to an end.

To want a man—a man they hadn't even met—as badly as she wanted to go into space blew her mind. No man should be a woman's dream. That was incredibly stupid. If love worked out within the carefully crafted framework of her career, then she was fine with it. Otherwise, no thank you.

The biodome had been retracted, leaving the small research station temporarily exposed while the rocket was tucked into the small courtyard between all the buildings. Margaret's whole body was jittery with excitement. She wanted to get off the rocket and explore everything. Maybe Jack Boyle would give them a tour. Against her most basic personality, she allowed herself to daydream about Jack showing them his biodome. He would be pointing out the advances in his lab (Margaret had already taken a virtual tour online months ago), then, mid-sentence, he'd see her through the crowd and pause to ask if he knew her from somewhere. Because even though she'd be in disguise, he'd know who she was right off the bat.

Margaret shook her head at her silliness. First, they'd only met for about two minutes in a hallway at a convention. And second, she couldn't believe she'd have a schoolgirl crush like this. She hadn't even behaved like this when she *was* a schoolgirl. Well, back then, all the guys were immature morons who didn't know an atom from a proton. But even the few men she'd dated in her life hadn't left her feeling jittery like this.

But instead of her imagined welcome tour of Research Station 7, they spent hours unloading boxes and setting up equipment. Margaret was only saved from this backbreaking duty when Lynette, who she'd heard ominously called either "The Handler" or "The Enforcer," summoned her into a small room one floor down. Two chairs faced each other, a camera and a large light on a stand crammed into one corner.

"Margo, we have a few quick minutes to film your backstory, since we didn't get it before we left." Lynette said, looking at her clipboard, her tone friendly and upbeat. "Thanks for being the last-minute fill in. Your brother said you were not to have any shots of gushing about how much you want to marry the bachelor, since you're slated to be voted off tomorrow."

"Thank God," Margaret said as she sat.

"None of that," Lynette said sharply, looking up from her notes.

Margaret blinked in surprise, watching the perky woman turn into something else entirely.

Lynette didn't seem friendly at all, but rather tough as nails. "You must stay in character at all times, since you might be in the background of other important shots and I can't have you messing those up."

"Okay," she said, surprised by Lynette's sudden shift in tone.

"I told your brother we would be better off one down, but he insisted on bringing you since it fulfills the deal he made with Station 7 in terms of numbers. I'm not going to have you go off the rails and infect the others with a bad attitude."

She was so harsh, Margaret sputtered out a laugh, but stifled it quickly when she saw the steel of command in Lynette's gaze. "Wow, you're a ball buster."

"Damn straight. You're not the only one acting on this trip. We all have to do our part to make good TV."

Margaret hadn't really watched TV since she spent most of her time in the lab, but she'd imagined the camera would follow them around while they went about their daily lives. "I thought this was supposed to be real?"

"It is. And you're going to make it extra real by staying in character." Lynette found the page she was looking for. "This is your backstory. You're from Raleigh, North Carolina and went to NC State University for biological and agricultural engineering. You live with two cats and play women's lacrosse in your free time. You're actually quite good at it. You volunteer regularly at an old folks' home."

"Wow," Margaret said again, horrified. Biological and agricultural engineering. What the hell was that? And lacrosse sounded dangerous. And two cats. Well she'd always wanted a cat. She just hadn't thought it was fair to an animal when she was always at work all the time. "Hank must be retaliating for that time I hemmed one of his tux legs an inch shorter before high school prom." It had brought her so much joy, but he'd promised to get her back when she'd least expected it. That time must be now.

Lynette gave her a look that was far from amused. "That's the backstory of the contestant you replaced. She's a real person who is quite sweet. You should take a page out of her book and get a better attitude." Lynette pushed a button on the camera and a red light came on. "First question, why did you want to come on the show?"

Relief coursed through her. This was an easy one. "Because it's filming on Mars."

"No. This is where you say you're at a point in your life you're ready for love."

"But—" Margaret wasn't at a point she was ready for love. Love was messy. And complicated. And from what she could tell, its primary purpose seemed to be distracting a good researcher from her purpose while screwing up her life.

Lynette growled. "Repeat after me. I'm ready for love."

"I'm ready for love," Margaret parroted. And, to her surprise, she found a small piece of her brightened at that statement, but the majority of her thought it was a stupid thing to say and from Lynette's disappointed frown, that part must have come through.

It went downhill from there.

Margaret tried not to be a jerk, but she wasn't an actress and she'd never been *light and bouncy* in her life. She wasn't even sure she knew what those words meant in relation to her own personality.

Over and over again, Lynette made her answer the same questions. "Smile! How hard is it to smile?" she asked at one point, throwing up her hands in frustration.

"Lynette," Margaret said, unable to take any more. "I'm not trying to make your life hell. I promise you." In fact, Margaret was starting to really like the other woman, who'd turned out to be smart and commanding. "I'm just not built for this."

Lynette slumped in her chair, looking more angry than defeated. "Your brother has screwed us both."

"I promised him and I'm promising you. I will try everything in my power to stay in character. But acting isn't something my brain can handle." Which was weird, actually, because Margaret had thought she could do anything she set her mind to. Turned out one of her personal mottos must have been wrong, because she couldn't act her way out of a paper bag.

Lynette studied at her for a long, assessing moment. "My gut says you're a major mistake. But we'll have to do the best we can." Lynette leaned forward in her chair. "I don't care how hard it is for you. You are no longer Margaret Carson. You are Margo Wilson, from Raleigh, North Carolina. I want you calling yourself Margo, even in your own mind. It is critical for you to give me everything you have for the next day." Lynette narrowed her eyes in a clear warning. "If you don't, your brother has told me to ban the testing of your rover."

"What?" Margaret gasped. To be on Mars and not test her rover would break her heart.

Lynette nodded and even appeared a little sympathetic. "Your brother seemed to think it was the only way to get full participation from you."

To have come this far and see her plans go up in smoke wasn't acceptable. Light and bouncy would be her middle name if it killed her. She pasted on a smile. "Margo from Raleigh it is," she said, the words a promise.

Lynette dropped her head in her hands. "Don't smile with your teeth showing. It makes you look like you're going to cut someone's heart out and eat it."

Margaret closed her lips.

Lynette peeked between two fingers. "Good enough."

They both went upstairs to find a guy named Russ wheeling clothes hanging from a long bar into the room.

"Okay, listen up," Lynette barked, holding her clipboard like a shield. "Your dresses for the first day's filming are on this bar with your names pinned to them. You are *not* allowed to switch dresses. You are *not* allowed to make any alterations to your dresses. You will wear what we've picked for you as they were given to you. *No* exceptions." She glanced at her clipboard. "You will be called in alphabetical order to the makeup room, which is down the spiral staircase in the first room on your right. You are *not* allowed to go to any other place on that floor. You will come straight back here after your makeup window is over. Please get dressed and be prepared for the start of filming, which begins in thirty minutes."

A general groan went through the room. They were all exhausted from the trip.

"You've been warned this season is going to have a grueling film schedule, so no whining. Jenny Armond, you're up."

Then Lynette stepped back and everyone but Margaret rushed to find their dresses, the room filling with a horrible din. The rack dwindled as the women fought to find their clothing.

Lynette caught Margaret's gaze and made a shooing gesture to encourage her to join the fray.

Margaret stepped up to the last remaining dress, her name pinned to the top of a long, pretty rose sheath. She pulled it from the rack, wincing at the sheer, delicate fabric that probably would tear like tissue paper. From a small bag clothes-pinned to the hanger, she pulled out extra control top hose, a strapless bra and some strings she suspected were supposed to be underwear. She spent a long time trying to figure out which holes were for her legs verses her waist. It was hard to tell.

"Margo Wilson," Lynette called from the top of the spiral stairs.

Margaret also wondered if the dress would even fit her, since she was wearing clothing meant for another woman. Holding the gown up to her body, she peered around another contestant into one of only two full length mirrors, and decided it couldn't possibly fit.

"Margo Wilson," Lynette called again, sounding super annoyed as she tapped Margaret on the shoulder. "Your makeup time is ticking away."

Relief filled her at the delay as she put the dress back onto the rack. *Margo. I am Margo*, Margaret repeated as she followed Lynette down to makeup and sat at the table that had been added to the same room she'd been interviewed in earlier.

The Enforcer studied her critically, before picking a bottle of foundation.

"You're the makeup artist?" Margaret asked in disbelief. Hank had assured her that she'd have the best and she figured she needed it. Further, Lynette wasn't even wearing any makeup. "I thought you were the person who does the interviews?"

"I'm everything on this shoot." Lynette dabbed a sponge onto Margaret's face, applying the liquid heavily. "Makeup artist, registration, handler, shrink, contestant wrangler, and enforcer."

"Are those all real titles?"

"No, but they're real staff positions."

"Shrink?"

"You'd be surprised. We have at least one person go whack every season." Lynette fell quiet as she powdered, brushed and started working on Margaret's eyes.

"Enforcer?" Margaret asked, unable to help it.

"Look up," Lynette ordered, drawing lines on the upper and lower lids. "Did you not read your contract? Because the list of behaviors that break your contract are long. And you're not going to be considered for *Paradise* if you break even the smallest of the rules."

"What's *Paradise?*" Margaret had fallen down the rabbit hole into a different world.

Lynette pulled back and studied her. "You aren't joking. Hank is so on my shit list." She tossed down the brush in obvious disgust. "It's the after show where everyone who didn't win has the chance to become even more famous by making complete asses of themselves on a tropical island. It's the golden ticket, much more coveted than this gig."

"Really?" Margaret was intrigued. It was like another world. One she knew her brother was suited for to a "T."

The Enforcer pointed an eyeliner at her. "And you won't go if you break the rules on this show, no matter how much of a fan favorite you are, so you better fly straight. I will not lose one second of sleep blackballing you if you fuck with me."

Margaret sat silent, too surprised to say anything in return. But Lynette didn't understand her at all if she thought banning Margaret from another show was a punishment.

"Lynette," Russ said from the doorway. "We have a problem."

"Here," Lynette said, shoving a new set of fake eyelashes into Margaret's hands. "Put these on. The glue is on the side table."

The other women left in a flurry of energy, leaving Margaret staring in the mirror. She was different, but really not different enough. She looked like herself, only better.

The package of fake eyelashes seemed to mock her as she studied them. Her name was on the outside of the case, so they had to be reusable. She turned over the box and revealed a set of directions. "Thank God," she whispered.

There were only three steps. How hard could it be?

Taking one out, she held it up to her lash line to measure them as the box instructed, and promptly poked herself in the eye. "Crap." She blinked rapidly to keep from messing up the eyeliner Lynette had so expertly applied.

This wouldn't defeat her. She had a PhD in mechanical engineering, dammit. This wasn't beyond her skills. Carefully following the directions, she trimmed the lashes to fit and put on the glue like an expert.

But despite her best attempts, the lashes ended up at her brow line or crooked or off to one side, like a caterpillar heading for her hairline.

"Need help?" the tall, gorgeous Tiffany asked, gliding in.

Margaret had met everyone before they'd left, but luckily they all still had nametags on, or she'd be lost. "Why is this so hard?" Margaret asked, peeling the offending item off.

"It just takes practice." Tiffany sat in Lynette's chair and took it from her. "Stare straight ahead and I'll do the rest."

Reassured by Tiffany's confidence, Margaret relaxed for the first time. "What do you do when you aren't on TV?" she asked, figuring Tiffany had to be a model.

"Focus on the wall behind me or your eyelashes flutter," Tiffany ordered, completely focused on the operation at hand.

Margaret stared at a filming schedule taped to the far wall, noting how many entries were listed under each day. These women would be working their butts off while they were here. Thank God she'd only have to endure the grueling schedule for a short time.

"I'm a social worker. Abused and neglected children." Two quick presses and the eyelash strip went into place on the first try.

Margaret leaned down to view them in the mirror. "Wow," she said, truly impressed by both Tiffany's deft skills and her job.

Tiffany popped the second lash from the case. "Last one." It went on just as easy.

"Wow," Margaret said again, peering close to the mirror. Her eyes were huge, filling her face. She looked younger, more innocent and… pretty. "I don't even look like myself," she whispered in awe.

"Fake eyelashes are amazing," Tiffany declared. "It's the most important thing in your vanity arsenal."

Margaret never had a vanity arsenal, but Tiffany almost made her wish she had.

"Let's go," Lynette barked from the top of the stairs. "Everyone! I need you in gowns and lined up in the hall in ten."

Tiffany snorted. "Time to practice exiting the rocket."

"We're going to practice walking down a ramp?"

"You know it. We'll practice everything. Haven't you watched the docuseries about the making of this show?" Tiffany lead the way to the changing area.

"No." Margaret was regretting she hadn't watched because it would've been helpful. If she'd had more time, she would have researched this. Or maybe she wouldn't, because she hadn't known how serious this whole thing had been until she'd been told testing her rover was in jeopardy.

Bolstering her courage, she prepared for an upcoming confrontation with Lynette when she couldn't fit into her dress. Because there was no way she was getting into it.

She stripped, managed to get the panties on, then struggled into the most soul sucking control top hose she'd ever worn in her life, then carefully drew the dress over her head. As expected, it stuck around her shoulders, but several other contestants rushed to her aid, pulling and yanking it down until the fabric settled around her, much to Margaret's surprise. The fabric had to have elastic in it. A lot of elastic.

She peered into the full-length mirror and was shocked to find the dress fit, even if it was tighter than anything she'd ever worn before.

The deep rose gossamer sheath hit the ground as if it had been handmade for her. With her hair twisted up, makeup on and this dress, Hank had been right. No one would ever recognize her.

She didn't even recognize herself.

But the excitement soon wore off because they spent the next two hours filming their walk from the rocket into the hallway connected to Boyle's laboratory. One by one, they went down the ramp, through a tunnel into Boyle's research center.

Margaret wasn't the only one who rapidly lost her patience with the process because Lynette spent the entire shoot yelling, "Smile!" and making everyone go back up the ramp to do it again.

Each time Margaret passed her, Lynette shouted, "Margo, please stop stomping. You need to float."

Margaret didn't know how to float and didn't want to know. Strangely, she'd thought she'd be nervous in front of the camera, but instead she was just aggravated. But she reminded herself about her rover, slapped on a smile, and tiptoed down the ramp, staring at a place beyond the cameraman's right shoulder.

Which obviously also wasn't floating, because Lynette said to Russ, "We'll have to edit her out," sounding put out and long-suffering.

By the end, Margaret was limping in her high heels and, because no one had bothered to feed them, starving. But the biggest annoyance was the fact that she hadn't seen hide nor hair of Jack Boyle.

CHAPTER THREE

I'm a spy. I'm undercover, Margo thought, using her spy name to refer to herself as Lynette had instructed.

She'd never really wanted to go undercover, but when she thought of it like that it seemed almost… fun.

And since she was a spy, she explored Jack Boyle's headquarters the moment Lynette was distracted by a filming snafu.

The tour didn't take long. Circling the round building, she ghosted from the lab into a hall full of storage lockers on one side and the second exit from the building on the other. The rocket crew had hooked a temporary, tarp-like structure to connect the building with the rocket, allowing the contestants to go back and forth without worrying about the outside temperature. A key upgrade, since they were dressed in almost nothing and while Mars might get up to 70 degrees during the day, at night it averaged minus 100, although the biosphere muted that when it was fully functional. Way too cold for an evening gown for sure.

From there, the hall ended in a tiny kitchen, which led to a living room where all the other contestants were sitting in a circle on the two chairs, the small sofa and the floor.

They were excitedly probing each other's backstories and sizing up the competition. As she wandered into what looked like Jack Boyle's bedroom, Margaret heard snippets of their lives more as a wash of background noise than a real conversation.

One woman was a veterinarian, one a social media influencer (whatever that was), another claimed to know the past winner of the *Paradise* show Lynette had told her about earlier.

The bedroom only had a bed in it and a few shelves with a small collection of rocks packing the surface. She picked up a dusty red pebble. It wasn't beautiful and she wondered why Boyle thought enough of it to keep it in his room on display.

Listening to everyone bonding in the main room, Margaret realized she'd never in her life been friends with women in the way that these women were rapidly becoming friends with each other. It wasn't that Margaret wasn't able to make friends—she could, just not easily and not with women. She hadn't had the practice. And really, who had time for casual acquaintances? Her life consisted of the lab, teaching, writing papers, writing grants (so many grants!) and sleeping when she could. She did better one-on-one than in a group anyway.

As she left Boyle's room, she caught a conversation about the bachelor Chad Harper. "Who is he?" she whispered to Tiffany, who stood against the wall beside Jack's room.

"Chad Harper?" Tiffany asked, incredulous to the point it came out on a huff of laughter.

Margo shrugged one shoulder as she nodded, hoping not to draw anyone else's notice.

"He was a finalist on *The Bachelorette*." Tiffany studied her as if to make sure her leg wasn't being pulled. "You know, the female version of the show."

Margo nodded, since that made sense. Bachelor. Bachelorette. She got it.

On the sofa, they all agreed that Chad was handsome and very sweet.

"He fell in true love with Cindy," one of the blondes said and the group nodded.

True love, as opposed to what? Fake love?

Margo realized someone had said her spy name and rewound the conversation in her head.

"What do you think, Margo?" the woman named Jenny had asked. They were all beautiful, but Jenny was a china doll, blonde and tiny and delicate, with an upturned nose and a soft-spoken southern lilt to her voice.

"Margo, you didn't say a thing the whole trip here," one of the two Black beauties commented. Her nametag, which they were still being forced to wear (thank God), said her name was Moni.

Margaret searched for something to distract the attention from her total lack of knowledge, so she asked, "You guys don't think Chad really loved Cindy, do you? I mean this *is* a TV show."

"*Of course* he loved her," a redhead named Misty said. "He *cried* when she didn't give him the final rose."

Margaret tried to keep the disbelief off her face.

"Oh, I know who she is," Amanda, a brunette, said, her voice full of wisdom. "She's the one who doubts the process, and gives all the interviews about how this isn't real and is totally a waste of time, then ends up falling the hardest. Like Jackie in season twenty."

Heads nodded in agreement, staring at Margaret, every gaze having a bit of criticism in it.

Margaret tried to stay in character. This wasn't the time to roll her eyes and say, *what's wrong with you people? This is TV. Of course, it's fake.* Instead, she said, "I don't watch a lot of TV," knowing she sounded lame, but she'd promised Lynette she wouldn't be negative.

"What do you do for a living?"

"I'm a scientist," Margaret said, wishing now she'd come up with a preplanned response to what her job entailed. Maybe the folder Lynette had given her listed it. She really should check that.

"Or maybe she's the brainy one," someone else said.

"*I'm* the brainy one," Claire informed them, her tone making it clear that she didn't appreciate the fact they hadn't noticed yet.

Margaret watched several women smirk and give each other looks.

For a second, she was transported back to middle school, where she'd been skewered by the other girls in her class. They hadn't let up until she accelerated out, skipping seventh and eighth grade to start high school two years early. It had been the biggest relief of her life. She'd never fit in once she'd gotten to high school, of course. She was too young to be friends with her new peers. But she hadn't been bullied either, her age making her an unsatisfactory target. She'd been much happier with that state of affairs.

Yet here she was, in middle school, a group of tigers circling her, waiting to pounce.

No, no, no, this was totally different. Soon, she'd be voted off and would spend another two days testing her rover, without having to talk to any of these women again.

Her distraction had worked, because the conversation had morphed into creating a list of all the couples who had really fallen in love on the show.

Margaret—no! her name was Margo, dammit. She'd slipped up there for a bit—wondered where Jack Boyle was and had a pang of sympathy that he would be forced to host them for the next few weeks.

Lynette marched in to send them off to touch up their makeup (*so much makeup!*) and climb into new dresses which had appeared hanging on a rack that now took up most of Boyle's laboratory.

"Okay, first group date will be Tiffany, Rose, Amanda, Misty, and Margo."

"That's a lot of people for a date," Margo muttered, wondering if she was going because they needed footage of her actually being a contestant. She'd hoped she wouldn't be picked for any of the close-up filming.

"That's better than usual where all but one of the cast go. Usually group dates are heavily attended. We must be in a tight space or doing an activity that can't handle a large group." Tiffany leaned over to peer into a shiny surface of a toaster-sized piece of equipment, creating a makeshift mirror. She carefully rubbed at the edge of her lipstick.

Margo was relieved Tiffany was filling her in. "But why so many of us?"

Tiffany raised one perfect eyebrow. "We can't fight over him if we aren't together."

Margo found the most intelligent thing she had to say was, "Oh." Well, *she* wasn't going to fight over a man. That would be ridiculous behavior. And unsavory.

They spent an hour filming themselves making dinner in the kitchen, a cramped ten-by-three-foot space that had the feel of a place where Jack Boyle made coffee and heated up premade food. *A man after my own heart.*

Lynette magically produced the ingredients for homemade pasta, tomatoes and spices for homemade sauce, and loaves of garlic bread that started as pre-shaped raw dough but smelled amazing in the oven. The wrangler seemed oblivious to how ridiculous it was to have a group of women in fancy dresses cooking dinner in a cramped kitchen on Mars, when there were so many other amazing things they could be doing. Like testing her rover. She could have a whole group date where she taught the women to drive it. She'd prided herself on making sure anyone could get behind the wheel with little to no training.

Margo might cook, but Margaret didn't, so she chose the task of chopping tomatoes and onions, since it sounded like something she couldn't screw up. She preferred to grab food at the University's cafeteria and eat in the lab while working late into the night.

She read the recipe as she diced, the directions so simple, even she could follow it. Really, she could do this at home. It wasn't hard at all and her basic nature enjoyed following the steps and accomplishing the tasks. She decided she would try the cooking thing back on Earth when she got home.

Someone touched her elbow, making the knife bounce dangerously close to her finger and Chad said, "Careful," his voice smooth and deep, like a radio host's. The Bachelor turned out to be tall, in great shape but not overly muscular, with black hair and sad light blue eyes. He immediately began chopping onions beside her, giving her an infectious grin. "So, what do you do, Margo?"

A strange flash of nerves finally hit her, reminding her of when she'd defended her thesis. She forced a smile, reminding herself that Margo was light and fluffy. And sweet, she added, thinking of Lynette's comments. There was no reason to be worried about the camera. This would soon be over in a few short hours and she could do all the things she'd come here to do. "I'm a biological and agricultural engineer." Before he could ask her what the hell that meant, since she really had no idea, she asked, "What do you do?"

"I'm a professional speed skater."

She blinked, having missed that detail before now. "As in ice skating?"

He grinned, obviously amused that she seemed to be hearing this for the first time. "Yeah."

"Like in the Olympics?"

"Exactly."

"That is really cool," she said, unable to stop the gushing. Because it was. Like being a finalist for a Nobel Prize.

"It's been amazing. I've had a ton of great coaches and my family is hugely supportive." He picked another onion.

Margo started chopping again, her mind whirling on the fact the bachelor seemed so normal and nice. She wasn't sure what she expected, but this wasn't it.

"Are you close with your family?" Chad asked her.

For a moment, she wondered if Margo was close to her family, but then figured it would be best to stick to her life story. "I am and I'm not. We're all super busy and we live in different towns, but I love them very much when it comes down to it. Even when my younger brother plays really mean tricks on me." She glanced at the camera in the corner. "He thinks he's funny but he's not," she added for good measure. There. Let Hank edit *that* out.

Chad paused mid-slice and gave her a sympathetic look. "How many siblings do you have?"

"Three." She realized that even if this was a game, Chad was a decent guy who seemed genuinely interested in getting to know her.

Chad placed a hand on hers and leaned close. "I've always wanted siblings, but I'm an only child."

She blinked at the contact, not sure she liked it, but she smiled at him as she knew Margo would. "I can't imagine not having siblings. I'm sure there are pluses to being raised alone."

"Chad," the redhead Misty called across the room. "Can you help me get this bread out of the oven? It's so hot!"

Chad turned away and Margo sighed in relief as the camera turned to someone else. "Sure," he said and dropped his knife. "It was great getting a chance to talk to you, Margo," he added.

"That wasn't terrible," she murmured as she watched him cross the kitchen, but she was glad to be out of the spot light.

When he leaned in to get the bread out of the oven, Misty gave Margo a close once over, her gaze saying, "hands off my man, bitch."

Margo turned back to her chopping but her peaceful culinary exploration was spoiled. Like she'd be happy with someone like Chad. The thought was ridiculous. As a speed skater, his life was all physical and hers all mental. They were polar opposites.

Things were easier from there. They only had to put together the simple meal and sit down to eat together. Since Margo was hoping to test her rover sooner than later, she left her filled-to-the-brim wine glass alone and drank copious amounts of water. The air was dry on Mars and hydration was key. Someone must have forgotten to tell the other contestants, because they were all quickly tipsy. But besides another few more warning looks from Misty, Margo was able to tune out the chatter and amuse herself by making a list of every experiment she planned to do while she was here. Things had been moving so fast, she really hadn't spent a lot of time thinking about that.

She was relieved when the group date was over and she could retreat to the lab, where she was hoping to find the mysterious Jack Boyle.

Instead, she found the camera guy, Russ, sitting in front of a bank of monitors, using a joystick to zoom in on Misty and

Chad, who seemed to be wrapped around each other in the kitchen pantry.

"Have you seen our host?" she asked Russ, trying to look away from the screen, where Chad was exploring Misty's tonsils.

"Nope. Asshole didn't even meet us when we landed." He zoomed closer to Misty's face, which was flushed with excitement.

"I cried for you when Cindy didn't give you the final rose, Chad," Misty said, and her expression of sympathy appeared real.

"Think all this is genuine?" Margo asked Russ, distracted for a moment by the thought that she was the only person acting. Misty and most of the other girls seemed to have bought into Chad as their potential mate.

"It is to some of them. Weirdest thing ever, but put people together under the stress we create, and it makes all kinds of things happen."

"This is stress?" They were on Mars, having an experience most scientists only dreamed about.

"If it isn't yet, it will be soon. Little sleep, competitions, the starvation they all seem to put themselves through, the threat of being sent home—this place will be a pressure cooker by the end."

He flipped to another screen and turned up the volume. The girls were sitting around on their camp beds inside the rocket.

"I'm just saying something's up with Margo. I saw her talking to Chad on our group date and it was like she was a different person," one said, her back to the screen so Margo wasn't sure who it was, but it sounded like it might be Rose.

"I've already called it. She's got the story line where they take her from doubter to convert," Amanda said. Or she thought it was Amanda. They weren't wearing their nametags anymore, so it was hard to be certain.

"They're on to you," Russ said.

Margo sighed. "Well, they aren't complete idiots." In fact, she was growing to like them. Or some of them. Tiffany had been nothing but kind to her. She'd still be trying to get those fake eyelashes on if Tiffany hadn't come to help.

"They aren't idiots at all." Russ toggled back to Chad and Misty. "We make sure we don't pick anyone with low IQs because the audience hates that. Everyone is at least above average. They're just desperate for love."

For a moment, she was distracted by Russ' lack of cynicism, but then she thanked the stars that she would never be so desperate. "Don't you think it's weird Jack Boyle isn't here?"

"Hank told us he's a first-class a-hole, so no. He probably can't fit us in with his busy schedule picking up rocks from the ground."

She opened her mouth to correct him, but then closed it, trying to honor her promise to Lynette to stay in character. *I am Margo. Margo would not correct Russ. Margo is sweet.* Who knew it would be this hard to be sweet?

"You better get back in there or Lynette will be on the warpath."

"Good advice," she said, and left quickly, not wanting to piss Lynette off when she held the keys to testing the rover.

Just in time, because it turned out that Lynette was right around the corner. "Margo!" she snapped, clearly starting to fray after a continuous filming cycle. The contestants had almost no sleep for the last twenty-four hours and neither had their handler. "We have a rose ceremony and you're not in the lineup."

Margo took a deep breath. *Sweet.* "Heading there now," she trilled in a perky voice, hustling into the tiny living room where they would all stand in a prearranged order. Sliding into her place between Misty and Amanda (earlier, Lynette had spent a long time distributing all the blondes through the group), Margo plastered a smile on her face, not wanting to get into more trouble.

Usually, the bachelor had someone like Hank there to be the master of ceremonies, but Lynette explained that they would digitally master him in when they returned to Earth. Hank wouldn't come until the second rocket in three days, which would bring the rest of their stuff and take home who-ever had lost up to that point.

Instead of Hank, they had Russ reading his parts. "So, um, how are you feeling about this process?" Russ asked Chad, his voice monotone and awkward.

"Russ," Lynette growled.

Russ looked up. "What?" he asked, puzzled.

Based on the sound of teeth grinding, Lynette struggled to maintain her cool. Not a good sign for the first day. "Just go on." She made a winding motion with her hand.

"How are you feeling about this process?" Russ asked again, a little faster this time but no less monotone.

Chad launched into an obviously pre-rehearsed speech that Margo immediately tuned out after he said he couldn't wait to find love.

Where was Jack Boyle? He was a recluse, but she would never let people in her laboratory unsupervised and she couldn't imagine he would either. Keeping the smile plastered on her face, she let her mind drift over everything she knew about the eccentric, brilliant geologist.

He was a legend, despite how young he still was. They had that in common, actually, both at the top of their professions, although he was certainly a bigger star to the non-scientific population than she was. He'd probably be better looking if he wasn't always scowling in every picture she'd ever seen. But his mind... his mind was so hot. She shivered.

Behind her, Jenny squealed and smashed into Margo's shoulder as she toppled off the highest riser on her way down. Chad had started giving out roses and Jenny was the first picked.

Why were these women here? They were all beautiful and, if Russ was right, they were above average intelligence. So, why do this? She watched Claire get her rose, so happy, the woman who claimed she was the brainy one cried.

Margo couldn't wait to be kicked off. The first thing she'd do would be change out of this gold atrocity they'd stuffed her into. She looked down for a moment at the strappy gold sandals peeking out below the matching dress. Her feet hurt so much and she knew she was one misstep away from falling on her ass. But, if she was honest, and she almost always was, she looked amazing. In fact, she was as beautiful as anyone else in the room. She just didn't care. For the most part. Okay, she supposed she cared a little bit. There was a hidden, girly part of her that might be pleased. She wondered briefly if Jack Boyle would find her beautiful. But even if he only found her rover beautiful, she'd be ecstatic.

Speaking of her rover...they'd parked it in one of the out buildings. That's where it had to be, because there was no place here for it inside this building. The thought of it had her straightening her back and plastering her smile back on. Lynette, standing behind one of the many cameras around the room, gave her a squinty-eyed glare and pointed her finger at Margo.

Margo relaxed her face as they'd practiced and clapped for Amanda as she went to get her rose.

Amanda and Chad kissed cheeks, as Amanda gushed out a yes to his question of would she accept the rose.

If Margo ever got a rose, which she wouldn't, she'd stride up there and say hell no and maybe stomp on the rose for good measure. She almost laughed out loud at the thought of her grinding a spiked heel into the delicate petals.

"Okay," Russ monotoned and stepped forward. "Only one rose left." It came out as one word, *onlyoneroseleft*, so Margo took a moment to decode it. Russ stepped back.

Margo realized only she and Misty remained rose free. Misty grabbed her hand and squeezed tightly. Margo would have patted her in reassurance because she knew Misty was staying, but she tried to stay in character and look worried.

"This has been such a hard choice," Chad said.

What a crock. We both know I'm first off. Margo tried to stop thinking so her face wouldn't get her in trouble with Lynette.

"It's so hard, since we've only had a short time together, but I really feel like I had an instant connection with one of you." Chad stared at them soulfully.

Straight at Margo. A spark of worry filled her.

He's just trying to make me feel better because I'm getting kicked off.

"But, Margo, I really want to get to know you better."

"What? No!" three people gasped.

Misty turned to her, flinging the hand away she'd gripped so hard. "You don't even want to be here," she accused, large tears gathering in her eyes.

"Misty, I'm so sorry," Margo said, so befuddled, she hugged the other woman, and she wasn't a hugger.

"Margo," Lynette hissed.

Margo turned and Lynette pointed to Chad meaningfully.

Oh my God, Margo thought. She wasn't kicked off. They'd promised her. *Promised!*

The other girls helped her off the riser and she hobbled the few feet to Chad.

"Margo," he said, his face so sincere, she almost thought he wasn't acting. "Will you accept this rose?"

For a moment, time stood still as a battle took place in Margo's brain. From the sidelines, Lynette waved and gestured, bouncing up and down on the balls of her toes, pointing at the rose and then making throat slashing motions.

My rover. If I say no, they won't let me test it. She knew Lynette wouldn't let her even see her vehicle if she messed up this filming.

But dang it, she wanted to say no. So. Badly.

She couldn't believe the lengths she had to go to for science.

All her earlier bravado fell away, and working harder than she'd ever worked in her life, Margo looked deep into Chad's sincere eyes and said, "Yes."

CHAPTER FOUR

*M*argo stood with Chad, Lynette and Russ in the lab. The rose ceremony had stopped when Lynette yanked them all back here.

"Chad, we talked about this," Lynette snarled.

"Yeah, well, Hank told me I had complete autonomy on who I picked in this process," Chad snarled back.

Margo blinked out of her brain freeze and really looked at Chad. Hands on his hips, his body a stiff, angry line, Chad wasn't backing down to Lynette. Whoa.

"You do, except for Margo. She is a stand in for the real Margo who couldn't come. You agreed to this back on Earth."

"Complete autonomy means I can pick who I want," Chad informed her. "Even if it's her."

"Wait," Margo interrupted. "Are you picking me just because Lynette told you not to?" She turned on Lynette. "Because if so, that's crap. We had a deal."

"Zip it, Margo," Lynette said, not bothering to look in her direction. "Chad, I know what Hank told you, but Margo isn't really Margo."

Margo would have laughed if she wasn't so pissed. Staying in the game meant that she had to do all the annoying things the contestants had to do. Which was a ton. The filming schedule alone left little time for sleep and equated to working their asses off.

When Hank had convinced her to come, she'd had no idea that she'd have to do so much, including moving furniture and boxes, setting up for shoots, and generally doing what a huge support staff must have done in the past. Just putting makeup on and doing hair took hours and was much more stressful than she'd ever imagined. "My rover—"

"You'll have plenty of time," Lynette cut her off, waving at her as if she were a fly. "Chad is going to vote you off tomorrow night."

"I will keep her if I want to." Chad's voice clearly said he would never let Margo go. Just to be a dick and screw Lynette.

"Wait a minute, you can't keep me just to spite Lynette. I made a deal to fill in that didn't include stuffing me into these ridiculous outfits and forcing me to be sickly sweet to everyone for longer than the first rose ceremony."

Chad turned to her, a mean light gleaming in his gaze. "Oh, yes I can."

Margo threw up her hands and stomped in a small circle to blow off some steam, although it wasn't very satisfying in the gold heels she wore, which were killing her. She longed for her tennis shoes and her lab coat. "I am testing my rover, people, for the record," she declared. When Hank showed up, she was going to kill him for doing this to her. She'd known this would all go horribly wrong. Known it!

She crossed the room to peer out the small window in the door, wondering which of the small outside buildings they'd stashed her rover in. Maybe she could sneak out somehow.

"Chad, don't be silly," Lynette said, her tone patient, as if she spoke to a child. "This is your chance to find real love. Do you really want to exclude a real contender to get back at me for locking you in your room all day yesterday?"

In the small window, a man's face suddenly appeared, distorted through his grey moonsuit helmet.

Margo jumped back, her gaze locking with his panic-filled eyes.

"Help," he mouthed.

"Oh my God." She raced to punch the release button to let him in.

The man fell forward without trying to catch his balance, his hands feebly scrambling on the floor.

Russ appeared beside her and helped her turn him over. "What's wrong with him?"

They dragged the man fully into the room so the doors could close.

The man floundered at the catches at his neck, his hands scrambling as he struggled, the skin of his lips an angry blue.

She pushed his hands away and flipped the latches, then wrestled off his helmet.

Jack Boyle curled onto his side, rasping in big gulps of air. He was older than her, thirty-five she knew, but he looked ancient, a bluish tint surrounding his lips and a rough day's growth of beard on his face.

She pointed to the screen attached to his wrist. "He was out of oxygen," she said to the group.

Chad and Lynette stood frozen beside her.

"We're in trouble," Jack gasped out.

"What kind of trouble?" she asked, the hairs on the back of her neck standing on end. Jack Boyle wouldn't panic. Whatever was happening had to be bad.

"The dying kind," he said. "You need to evacuate immediately."

Jack blinked, wondering if he was hallucinating from lack of oxygen.

The blonde woman barely dressed in a gold floor-length gown propped her hands on her hips. "I'm not going anywhere without running my tests," she snarled.

Jack shook his head, trying to make some sense of the words. All he could think about was the fact that the same people who took out his rover—he'd begun to think it was the Russians because the Chinese wouldn't be so obvious—could be on their way to Station 7. And that meant he had to get these people out of here, pronto, before he ended up with a bunch of dead debutantes on his hands.

He tried to wrap his mind around the odd group staring down at him. The two men were polar opposites. One looked like he stepped out of an ad for six-figure watches, the other a poster child for aging video gamers everywhere. The two women weren't very similar either, but he figured the one in the full-length dress had to be a contestant on the idiotic show they were filming. What was all this about tests?

"Are you hard of hearing? I said you need to evacuate. Someone vaporized my rover and they may be heading here."

"I'm not going anywhere." She turned to the other women, dismissing him. "Lynette, Chad can keep me in the game as long as he wants, but I'm testing my rover. Period."

"No one is leaving," Lynette answered, a finality in her words that meant she was the one in charge.

Despite being completely exhausted from hours traveling on little oxygen, Jack sat up. "Are you people deaf? Someone blew up my vehicle and left me hiking six hours back to the station. By all rights, I should have died. Hell, I almost did. You need to get out of here before they attack the station."

"Someone who?" Goldie asked, leaning down to catch his shoulder when he started to tip backwards.

He shooed her away. "I don't know. Maybe the Russians."

Goldie's blond hair swept into a twist on her head and her face had the delicate, carefully bred features of a super model. But she wasn't *acting* like a super model. She was acting like a large pain in his ass.

"Or possibly the Chinese, although it seems too aggressive for them," he conceded. "The craft wasn't like anything I've seen before," he said, staggering to his feet and over to the console. "The U.S. Government recently warned that both were moving to establish a presence on Mars for their countries, but I'd thought they were just setting up their own research stations. More information was supposed to be forthcoming but I guess things were put in play sooner than they'd thought."

He typed: *Rover blown up by hostile forces in an unknown aircraft with no markings. Evacuating cast of show immediately.*

He sent the message to his NASA contact.

Lynette smacked her clipboard onto the lab table. "Listen, Boyle, you promised us a place to film and we paid you good money *up front* to get one."

"I think any lawyer on Earth would agree I can't control the Russians attacking the planet."

"You're pulling the Act of God clause?" Lynette's voice was incredulous, but he didn't try to soothe her.

"You bet I am. I'm not having your deaths on my hands." His plan was simple. Get rid of the cast and stay here to defend his station.

"I'm not leaving," Goldie said again.

"No one is leaving," Lynette said, clearly under the impression she was still in charge.

"All of you are getting out of here as fast as we can load up that rocket out there. I'm not going to have a bunch of dead civilians on my hands." He had thought about it the whole walk home. If he made it here alive and the station hadn't been attacked yet, he'd bundle the cast up and send them home. Since it was an act of God, he would be free of them and could keep the money.

Then he'd find whoever was out there and lay some traps. He'd blow up his station before he'd let it fall into anyone else's hands. For the first time since he left the army, Jack had the burn to fight.

But first, he had to document what was happening so those on Earth could avenge him if he wasn't victorious.

"No one is leaving because no one *can* leave," Lynette said.

"What?" Jack froze, his hands mid-motion as he typed another message.

"We didn't bring enough fuel for a return trip."

"What?" Jack asked again, this time louder, because he couldn't believe his ears.

"To get all the items here we needed for filming, we had to reduce the fuel on board down to nothing. We barely had enough to make it up here."

He couldn't believe it. "You did what?" he had to ask again. These people were driving him to reiterate.

Lynette shrugged.

Jack swung past her. "Where is that idiot Hank Carson?"

"Um, he had to stay back, too," Lynette said.

"Hank's not an idiot," Goldie said, so huffily that Jack figured Hank must be her boyfriend.

"He didn't come to his own TV show? What kind of operation are you people running here?" He waved off the two women's answers. "It doesn't matter and frankly, I don't care," he said, trying to think.

The calendar on the wall said it was the beginning of the month. Then it came to him. Walter Haxley might have a supply shuttle coming to Station 5.

For a second, Jack didn't want to ask Haxley for help. If it had only been to save his own life, he'd die before he begged Haxley for a favor. They'd been rivals all of Jack's career. But he had a bunch of civilians here, trapped, and he had to be a bigger person if he was going to save them.

He brought up the communications unit and paused again, because he *really* didn't want to call Haxley. They'd hated each other since Jack had won a grant right from under Walter's nose and he'd retaliated by calling Jack a third-rate rockhound.

But Jack's gut told him now was not the time to quibble over past slights. His gut told him whoever had blown up his rover was coming here next. In fact, he couldn't believe they hadn't already arrived.

He threw the switches and typed the commands.

His Spidey sense screamed at him to get them out while he still could. But where could they go? There wasn't any place to hide.

When he made it to the lab, he should have been home free, but his hands hadn't been working right when he'd punched the code into the door and he'd errored out. He suspected he'd been fat fingering his code in the haze of hypoxia. Maybe he had been hallucinating and never actually hit any numbers at all. He'd looked through the small window to see an angel staring back at him. She'd obviously had enough sense to punch the button to let him in, although he wasn't sure how intelligent she was now that he'd met her.

He was lucky he hadn't died a single step from his lab.

Lynette pushed past Goldie, trying to take back command. "If we're in trouble, what are *you* going to do about it?"

"Everyone quiet," Jack barked, sick of the harping.

He connected to the satellite. A steady ping began, lasting for over ten minutes. Goldie came closer and scanned the control panel, as if it made sense to her. Which was silly, since Jack figured anyone who went on these shows had to be a moron.

Finally, after what seemed like a short lifetime, Haxley answered. Only it wasn't the usual, arrogant face Jack was used to. Walter's face was covered with black smudges and his eyes were huge and filled with fear. "Jack! Jack! You called."

"Yeah," Jack said, a bad feeling creeping up his spine as he realized that they—whoever "they" were—weren't here yet because they were taking care of Station 5 first.

"Our long-range transmissions are disabled. I didn't even think to try to contact you. We'd just assumed the feed had been cut." Haxley looked behind him at someone off screen, his actions nervous and jittery. "Our rovers were all destroyed by long-range missiles. My tech guy died in the electrical shed trying to patch through to Earth. It's just Ellen and me left."

Oh shit. We're all going to die.

Jack took a deep calming breath, stuffing down the uncharacteristic punch of panic. *No, no we aren't. I've got this.* "Do you know who's behind the attacks?" Jack asked, although did it matter? Russia or China, they were still dead if they didn't get outside help. *Know your enemy is a motto for a reason. You can't fight what you don't understand.*

"No. We haven't even laid eyes on any of them, but this must have been what the CIA warned us about last month."

"The CIA said there were plans for China and Russia to land teams here, not for them to sabotage our stations."

Haxley shrugged off his point. "It looks like they want to take the buildings intact and they're going to starve us out."

They were going to be under siege. And he had fifteen new mouths to feed. Shit. "Do you have a supply shuttle coming any time soon?"

"No. It won't be here for two weeks."

Two weeks would be too long. "My shuttle should come in the next couple days, I'll let them know your situation. I've sent a message, but you know how that goes out here." Communication all depended on not running into any sun spots and atmospheric storms.

Haxley's gaze sharpened. "When exactly is your shuttle coming?"

"Sometime this week," Jack hedged, not sure why he was reluctant to say, but following his gut. If the Russians had tapped into their communications, then they would know too. "Listen, Walter, I have to go," he said, cutting their conversation off, because he still had a big problem on his hands he had to solve.

"Was *that* your idea of help?" Lynette said, her voice filled with anxiety.

"Would it make more sense to combine forces, invite him here to hunker down with us?" Goldie asked.

The thought of Haxley at Jack's station made his skin crawl. "It makes more sense to force the opposition to spread out to keep us both locked down."

Lynette stomped closer. "Why don't you call someone on Earth?"

"In case you haven't noticed, there are no phones. AT&T hasn't set up shop here. I'm sending messages now." Technically, he could call if the rotation of the planet was in the right alignment. Usually, the lag was so extreme it wasn't worth trying to have a conversation. It took four to twenty-four minutes for a message to reach Earth from Mars, then the same amount of time to come back.

Lynette's mouth opened and closed a few times as she started to argue with him, but the reality of their situation must have sunk in. "Oh my God, we're going to die," she moaned.

Jack tried to tune her out. He needed a new plan. Quickly, he typed another message to Earth. If they were cutting communications, then he might only have a small amount of time to get more messages out. It was also possible that his rover had just gotten caught up in an attack on Haxley's Station, although from the location he'd been in, that seemed unlikely. He was so far north from Station 5, he shouldn't have attracted notice.

Behind him, the heavy guy with a ponytail and goatee said, "I knew I shouldn't have signed up for this shit. Hank always talks me in to joining his crews, but I had a feeling Mars was going to be a bust."

"Don't panic," Goldie said, her voice firm and in control. "There is always a solution. Jack Boyle will get us out of here."

Her tone held so much blind faith, Jack turned to gape at her. "Who are you?" he asked, because why was she even in the lab? None of the other contestants were.

"She's Margo Wilson," Lynette said, the words rushed, like it was important.

Goldie harrumphed at that.

Something weird was going on but Jack didn't have time to focus on it. "Whatever. All of you be quiet."

He finished a longer message and put everyone he could think of on the distribution list, and pressed send.

Then he tried to come up with a plan, but no brilliant ideas came to mind. The best he came up with was the obvious need to get everyone away from any means of transportation since the Russians seemed to be blowing them up. Besides, pulling them into one location was like his own version of circling the wagons. "I've done what I can. Now, we need to move everyone off the rocket."

"That's not possible," Lynette said. "The contestants can't cohabitate in the same building as the Bachelor."

Jack wondered how his reality and the one the TV people lived in could be so different.

"Listen, we're in the middle of a crisis. We need to pull in food from the outside huts and stack it here. If they trap us in this building, then we'll need to have supplies to sustain us until a rescue ship arrives." *If* they sent a rescue ship. Which they might not. The shuttle coming in a few days was worth a lot of money. Would they risk it to save a few lives? That shuttle was his resupply company's only rocket.

He couldn't think like that. In fact, he wouldn't. The death of hope led men to be sloppy.

"We're living on the rocket," Goldie said. "Everything we have is out there."

"The first thing they'll do when they focus on this station is take that rocket out. Or at least, that's what I would do if I was on the other side, so we have to get ready for that. They don't know it has no fuel in it." Man, that chapped him. "What on Earth were you thinking?"

"We were thinking we had a major last-minute addition to our weight requirements." Lynette gave Goldie a significant look.

"I had no idea," Goldie whispered.

Lynette shook her head, as if she were waking up from a nightmare. "Never mind. The contestants are not allowed to see the Bachelor when we aren't filming. That's an unbreakable rule."

"Lady, in case you haven't gotten the memo, we've got a situation here," Jack said, understanding for the first time exactly how horrible this was going to be for him. It was like these people were from another planet.

CHAPTER FIVE

*I*t occurred to Margo, as she watched Lynette and Jack Boyle arguing about the Bachelor being in contact with the contestants, that she was both horrified by how rude he was and completely impressed by his ability to hold firm in the face of Lynette's arguments. She leaned against the console as she watched them, resting first one foot, then the other. The two of them weren't backing down and no one seemed to be budging anytime soon. She imagined them both still standing in the same position ten years from now, only their skeletons remaining.

Soon growing bored of their argument, Margo carefully eased into the chair before the console, hoping not to rip the gold dress that was a smidge too tight. She really should work out more. Or maybe stop eating chocolate. And the wine could probably go too. But then she thought *screw that* and took off a shoe to knead her right foot, which hurt a little more than the left.

Boyle's face had turned a vibrant shade of red. "I'm in charge of this station, and I'm telling you all to move your things in here and get ready to hunker down."

Behind him, Russ slowly drifted backwards toward the door, one step, then another, then he stepped sideways and was gone. Margo grinned.

Letting her gaze drift to the console, she admired the sleek, modern lines of it. The designer had obviously been going for the standard TV starship command center look, with a bunch of buttons and small screens surrounding two much larger ones. Her gaze drifted to one of them and she noticed an error box.

ERROR NO SATELLITE CONNECTION—NO MESSAGES WERE SENT

Uh oh. "Um, Jack," she said.

"You don't seem to be understanding the seriousness of this situation," Boyle growled to Lynette, ignoring Margo.

"I'll tell you what I think of your situation—"

"Guys," Margo yelled, clapping her hands once.

Lynette jumped and Boyle's laser focus swung to her.

She pointed to the console. "Your message failed."

"Let me see." He stomped over and let out a curse.

She waved a hand at the screen like a game show hostess showing a prize, wondering just how bad things really were. Her brother would show up in three days on the shuttle. They had more than enough food to last them until then. When Hank landed, they could simply climb into his rocket and return to Earth.

"Out of my chair," Jack ordered.

She put on her shoe and stood, appalled at how rude he was. His mother should be ashamed for raising him like this. Although maybe that was the issue. Perhaps he'd been raised in a pack of wolves.

It was not hot. At all.

Her feet protested, screaming at her. She thought she heard them saying Jack Boyle is a jerk. Devastation at the loss of her daydream washed over her. He was still hot and still a genius, but he wouldn't do as dream fodder. It annoyed her that he'd ruined it.

He plunked down and scrambled across the keyboard, punching the keys, muttering under his breath. Finally, he leaned back in her chair. "They've cut our coms. We're well and truly fucked." He pointed his finger at Lynette. "Move everyone and everything you brought into the main room. I want it done on the double."

For a second, it appeared Lynette was going to argue again, then she changed her mind. "Go pack your stuff, Margo, including your cot. I'll get the other girls moving."

Margo didn't need to be told twice. All she wanted was to change into a pair of jeans and get out of these shoes. No emergency should be met in a floor-length gown.

From the side door, she hustled down the temporary hallway from the ship to main building, taking off her heels so she could move fast. When she reached the room she shared with the contestants, she had her dress off and real clothes on in a heartbeat. Then she shoved all her personal things in her bag, put on her hiking boots, and collapsed her camp cot. She gathered up everything right as all the rest of the women entered. She zigged around them, trying to slip out as the last person came in.

Misty held out her arm across the doorway, barring Margo's escape. "What the hell was that, Margo?"

"We're being filmed, Misty, so watch your tone," she whispered, not wanting to get the other girl in trouble or have either of them featured on TV sniping at each other. She'd watched all of twenty minutes of another of Hank's shows and the whole time, women seemed to be fighting over just about anything and everything. It had been beyond painful and she didn't want to turn into a highlight.

"I don't give a shit if we're being filmed," Misty snarled, rising up to her full height, which was taller than Margo's 5'9".

"Misty, don't." Amanda tried to pull her arm off the doorframe. "Chad picked Margo. It's not her fault."

"Come off it, Amanda. You know she was supposed to be voted off. She wasn't even trying." Amanda gave her a head-to-toe appraisal. "I mean, she doesn't even know how to put on strip lashes. I saw Tiffany teaching her."

"Well, they're really tricky," Margo defended herself, but she was supposed to go home. "I tried my best on this show."

"Did you see her when we were cooking? Cuddling up to Chad, fluttering her eyelashes," Misty said, stepping closer, giving a series of exaggerated blinks that looked ridiculous. Then she raised both fisted hands, like she was going to fight.

Oh my God, someone is going to fight me. Like they were on some talk show that revealed who the Baby Daddy was. Margo tried to close her mouth, which had fallen open.

Amanda pulled on Misty's arm again. "She won fair and square, Misty."

Margo woke up out of her shock. "I wasn't cuddling up. But even if I was, that's the point, isn't it? To get Chad to like me?"

"She's right. That's what we're here for. I told you, Margo's the stealth contestant and she stealthed you, Misty," Claire said from across the room, a bit of satisfaction in her tone, because Misty wasn't popular with the other women.

The other contestants had stopped packing and stared at Margo, considering her like this was a real possibility.

Margo wanted to explain to them that she was just here to test her rover, but they were being filmed. And Lynette would be pissed if she ruined the fight scene.

And then, like a ton of bricks, it hit her. This whole Russian attack could be some elaborate scheme to put them under more pressure so Hank would get good film clips. "We need to go. Boyle said we had to be moved as fast as possible." She zigged quickly to the right and got around Misty before she could put her arm up to block her again.

Misty lunged but was no match in her heels to Margo's hiking boots even with Margo being weighted down with all her gear. Margo broke into a run, her anger giving her speed.

Returning to the main building, Russ pointed to the living room. "Set up your bed in there. Lynette is putting together a new filming schedule."

"New schedule?" she asked, all her suspicions gaining strength. "Aren't we in the middle of a crisis? Or is this some sort of setup to put us under more stress?" She studied Russ' face, trying to see if he gave anything away.

Russ shrugged, but pursed his lips as if he was considering it. "If it's a set up, they haven't told me."

Margo believed him. Russ just wasn't equipped to lie.

"Which has happened before, now that I think about it."

"Wait, they do things without letting the staff know?" She had a hard time believing that.

"It makes things more authentic if whatever happens comes as a surprise for us too. That way we can't telegraph to the contestants what is going on. We had a contestant that was an actor hired to create major drama on My Girlfriend 4 and I never knew a thing until she was voted off."

Well, if this was some sort of elaborate set up and she didn't get to test her rover, Hank was a dead man walking. Margo stalked into the living room, so mad, she took the little alcove that was clearly the best spot in the room. Until she tested her rover, she wasn't participating in this bullshit and she'd tell Lynette that, too. Because it was only Boyle's word that his rover had been blown up. And who would blow up a rover here on Mars? No one, that's who. It didn't even make sense. The Russians had most of a planet to set up shop.

Some of the girls streamed in while she silently fumed, her mind going back and forth over what one minute was the most outlandish conclusion she'd ever come to (after all, this was Jack Boyle she was talking about here—was he capable of an elaborate falsehood?) and her brother's well known deviousness.

It occurred to her that she should just find Boyle and ask. He wasn't an actor. He wouldn't be able to lie under her scrutiny. She marched to the lab, ready to do battle.

He still fiddled with the console, trying to get his communications up and running, testing wires to see if one had come unplugged.

"Boyle," she said, taking her no-nonsense tone she used with errant undergrads. "I want to know exactly what you saw out there."

"Who are you?" Jack asked again, not even bothering to turn her direction.

What did he mean, who was she? She was Margaret Carson.

No, actually she wasn't. She was Margo Wilson, who would never challenge Jack Boyle. She would probably hide from this man, totally intimidated. Well screw it, she wasn't going to be Margo until she had some answers. "You just met me," she said, feeling her temper expand a little more. Because they had stood here an hour ago and Lynette had introduced them.

He looked up. "Oh, right, the one who lied about her name." He returned to his computer fiddling.

"I didn't lie. I never told you my name. That was Lynette. And anyway, you weren't supposed to know that it's fake." She didn't let him pull her off course. She was here for a reason.

"You aren't a very good actor."

She threw her hands up in the face of this unexpected confrontation. "No. I'm not. I don't want to be an actor."

"Then you shouldn't have come on this show."

A growl of frustration filled her chest. "No, I shouldn't have," she agreed, wondering if violence was the answer here. Perhaps it was, because, for the first time in her life, she wanted to hit someone. Jack Boyle, specifically. "What I need to know is what you saw out there."

That got his attention. "Why?"

"Humor me."

He pointed to his console. "I'm in the middle of something important."

When he started to turn away again, she grabbed his arm.

And something odd happened. A small shiver went through her. Because his bicep was rock hard, like he lifted weights, and his body was so warm, she wanted to press into him. She'd been terribly cold since she got here.

She snatched her hand away. "Just tell me what you saw."

"Why?"

"Because I think this might be a set up. An elaborate ploy for TV ratings."

"My rover was blown to smithereens."

"You saw it?"

"Damn straight I saw it."

Okay, so Jack Boyle wasn't involved. But what if he was just as big of a patsy as all of them were? "What if the show blew up your rover for the ratings boost?"

For a moment, his mouth compressed and a storm gathered in his eyes. The air tightened with the force of his building wrath. Then he shook his head. "First, the other ship wasn't anything

I'd seen before. No way Carson has access to something I haven't at least heard about. And second, if Hank Carson blew up my million dollar rover for a stunt for his show, I will personally cut his liver out of his body."

"Yikes," she said, wondering if he really would do that. The steel in his gaze said he might. Boyle was tough as hell and ready for a fight, that much was for sure. She found that oddly reassuring. In a crisis, it was good to have a warrior on hand. "You're sure it was a foreign ship?"

"Matte black, conical. And my rover took a direct hit that didn't even destroy the rocks around it. One minute I had a rover, the next I had a pile of dust. No way the show had anything to do with that."

"They might have set explosives," she said, trying to think it through.

"And leave me out there without enough oxygen to make it back? You really think your boyfriend would do that?"

"What boyfriend?" She hadn't dated anyone in years. Men were too big of a distraction.

"Carson."

Eww. She was insulted he thought she'd fall in love with someone so flighty, let alone that that someone was her own flesh and blood.

But would her brother have done it? She shook her head, discarding the whole conspiracy theory. "No, you're right. Even for Hank that's over the top," she agreed. Besides, his attorneys wouldn't let him risk someone's life. She was pretty sure. Unless they'd had Boyle sign a release?

Still, she wasn't completely convinced. Her brother was pretty focused when it came to getting high ratings, and he had said he was going to win an Emmy with this. "Still, you didn't die, did you?" He'd made it inside with just enough oxygen to spare.

"What?" Jack asked.

"Margo, what are you doing in here?" Lynette snapped from behind her, making Margo jump. "The cast is in the living room."

She returned to character and tried to smile and be sweet. The real Margo would apologize, so she did. "Sorry, Lynette." Being Margo was so hard. She couldn't wait to get back to Margaret. "Only three days until Hank gets here," she said out loud, relieved for once that her brother would arrive soon.

"Carson is going to fly right into a trap if we don't find some way to warn him," Jack growled, focused again on his console.

"What?" Margo was confused. "What trap?"

"If they destroyed my rover, they'll destroy his rocket."

"They aren't going to destroy his ship," Margo informed him.

"Yes they are."

She shook her head. "If they were, they'd have blown it already."

He stood up, right into her personal space. "I'm telling you, they are going to disable all vehicles like they did to Haxley."

He made her so mad, with his commanding, bossy tone, she wanted him to be wrong, just on principal. She stepped into his space. "Last I looked, it was still in one piece."

From outside a massive snap sounded, knocking everyone off their feet, sending Margo stumbling into Boyle. He pin-wheeled his arms trying to keep them both standing, but gravity got the better of him and he hit the floor. Unable to catch her balance, she landed on top of him.

He let out a loud, "Oof."

"Oh my God," she said, her body draped across his.

He was a lot more in shape than she expected, even with the earlier preview of his bicep. The lean muscle was hard beneath her. She blinked at his nearness and the fact that she didn't hate him after all. In fact, she might want him. Sexually. Because her libido, which she'd thought had packed up and headed for Siberia a long time ago, suddenly sat up and purred *yummy*.

For a moment, their gazes caught and she thought *he's going to kiss me!*

Then an alarm started blaring.

He reversed their positions easily, rolling her to the floor and got to his feet. Offering her a hand, he pulled her to standing with ease, then steadied her as she tried to stiffen her jellied limbs. Wow. She felt like she'd been hit by an anvil. Who knew grumpy old Jack Boyle could light her fire?

With sigh that told her he was too busy to help her stand any longer, he plunked her in the chair, then fiddled with the screens until he shut off the alarm and brought up a camera view of the outside.

Oh right. The explosion. She'd forgotten with the lust explosion of her own.

The rocket they'd arrived in was smashed to pieces in the courtyard, almost as if she'd jinxed it with her comment.

"Oh no," Lynette moaned. "That had all our supplies in it."

"You didn't move them out?" Jack asked, incredulous.

"I hadn't had time to organize everyone to get them. I'd just had the contestants move their camp beds and personal items."

"But a hit that would make the rocket disintegrate like that should have caused a shock wave that knocked us all into oblivion," Margo said, truly puzzled as she stared at the camera view. The rocket was only a hundred feet away from the building.

Boyle shook his head as he clicked through some other panels. "It should have, but it didn't. Even the biodome took such a small hit that it's trying to reseal itself."

"What happened?" Russ asked from the doorway. Behind him, a bunch of women tried to peer over his shoulder, a sea of blonde, with the occasional brown, black and red dotted into the mix.

"There has been an explosion," Lynette said, falling into her role as if she hadn't been losing it before. "Everyone is to stay in the living room. We're still taping, so look sharp." She herded them out of the room, waving her arms. "Why don't we have a Tell All Session?"

"What's a Tell All Session?" Jack asked Margo, mimicking Lynette's emphasis on the words.

"When they gripe about not spending enough time with Chad," Margo said, knowing they would edit her response out, not wanting any of their secrets escaping.

"What exploded?" Russ asked, coming fully into the room.

"Your ship." Jack pointed to the computer screen, where his camera swept through the biodome, seeing nothing but intact buildings all around what looked like a mound of dirt, but was in fact the disintegrated rocket.

Russ peered at the screen, his eyes growing bigger. "Wait," he said, his voice full of dread. "I think there were still people in there." When they looked at him without comprehension, he clarified. "In the rocket. I think some of the contestants were still out there."

⌐——————⌐

The handler, Lynette, lost it and had to be placed shaking in the same chair he'd just put Goldie in, so Jack organized the headcount.

"I've lost contestants. That's the number one death knell of a handler. I'll never be employed in reality TV again," Lynette whispered over and over, rocking back and forth on the chair.

Goldie, on the other hand, was still with him, strong and willing to help in her hiking boots and jeans. "I'm going to kill Hank," she whispered, over and over again, taking comfort, Jack supposed, in the thought she'd still be alive to do so. She seemed like a together woman, so he wondered why she was dating a clown like Carson. But he supposed that's what women did. Date jerks. It wasn't like he'd ever understood the female of the species.

Lynette wasn't the only person losing it. Jack must be going off his rocker too, because he almost kissed Goldie when she fell on him. He shook his head. Yeah, she was hot, but she wasn't his type. He didn't date women who owned full-length gowns and looked like models. He dated other scientists or university administrators. Or he had before he'd come to Mars.

They left Lynette rocking back and forth, muttering. Jack had seen people break down like this before. It might be temporary, or it might be something she wouldn't recover from.

"Everyone to the living room immediately," Jack yelled at the top of his lungs. He wasn't looking forward to figuring out who had been in the rocket when it was blown to bits. If anyone had been out there. He reminded himself they didn't know yet.

He entered the living room, Goldie and the camera guy trailing him, and told everyone to sit. They sat on command, surprising him. He was used to big egos that wanted to lead, not people following orders. "Okay, camera guy—"

"Russ," he said.

"What?"

"That's my name. Russ."

People always were so caught up in names. "Russ," he conceded. "Do a roll call. How many of them are there, anyway?"

"Twelve," Goldie said. "Thirteen with the bachelor."

Russ counted, then recounted. "We're short five."

"Oh no!" a blonde screamed, making Jack jump. "Chad! Chad isn't here."

All the women started screaming, a loud, piercing sound that would put a coed in a horror movie to shame.

Jesus Christ on a stick. His nerves weren't going to last through all this.

"Quiet," he yelled, making even Goldie flinch beside him. "Let's do a complete check before we hit the panic button." Maybe Chad was off somewhere with one of the women having sex. Maybe he was with all of them, doing a fivesome. Part of Jack hoped so. He couldn't take more screaming. "Russ, you and Goldie check the building and make sure no one else is here. I'll run through all the outbuildings just in case they happened to end up in one."

Jack had a bad feeling about this.

CHAPTER SIX

*M*argo and Russ split up the main building. She took the side hall from the lab and he started in the living room. The small, round building wouldn't take long to search.

"Meet you in the middle," Russ called, his urgency bringing him into an almost-jog.

They'd decided that they would open anything large enough for a person to fit into, so Margo searched the ten lockers along the hall that held space suits and other supplies. Open, look, shut, open, look, shut, her tempo increasing speed as she went.

Taking the elbow turn, she quickly opened a closet, took a fast glance and shut. And stopped.

She stood still, her mind stuttering on what she'd just seen.

Then she opened back up the closet.

"Do you mind?" Misty screeched, her creamy skin gleaming in the dim light of the closet, her breasts bouncing.

It was the position they were in that had tripped Margo's brain. "What are you doing?" she asked without thinking.

"Reverse cowboy," Lynette hissed behind her, then pushed into the small space.

At the sight of the handler, Misty tried to scramble off, but Chad was holding her hips, still thrusting away.

Lynette smacked her hand on the wall, causing the metal structure to clang. "Which is expressly listed as not allowed during filming."

Misty toppled forward as Chad sat up, dislodging her.

"Lynette, I can explain," he sputtered, grabbing for his pants, which were under Misty's knee.

He gave another, huge tug, making Misty tumble over. "Hey!" she snarled, tossing him a furious look.

Lynette put her hands on her hips, her small stature growing with her rage. "You've breached your contract, buddy. Hank is going to have your head on a pike when he gets here." Lynette turned to Misty, who was trying to get her dress back on. "And you are out!"

"I was already out, you fat cow," Misty said, struggling to get her gown over her sweaty body.

"Cow, am I? Well mooooove the hell out of this closet and go sit on the floor in the lab next to the exit door where I can keep an eye on you. If your ass so much as shifts an inch, you'll be on bathroom cleaning duty for the duration on this hellhole."

Margo glanced away as Chad pulled on his pants, not bothering with underwear.

"Oh go fuck yourself, Lynette." Misty stood half-naked in all her righteousness, her dress stuck at her waist. Then she turned her back to show them a large tattoo on her ass. Pink heart with words scrawled across it. Margo didn't lean in to read them.

"You just lost your shot at being Paradise, bitch. Think I can't make that happen, think again."

Misty pushed her lower lip out in a pout while she tried to straighten her dress.

"Oh my God," Margo whispered, taking a step further away and bumping into Russ, who seemed to be enjoying the view.

"I have a camera set up in here," he said to Lynette.

"You perv!" Misty blew by them all, her underwear crumpled in her hand.

"You won't use that film, will you?" Margo asked, horrified.

"No," Lynette said. "Because Chad can't be compromised." She held a finger out to him. "You do that again, Chad, and I'm docking your money."

"You can't do that!" he huffed.

"I can and will, because this is so clearly excluded in the contract, you would never even get a lawyer to represent you, let alone fight it."

He opened his mouth to argue.

"It's ironclad. You're going to spend the next few hours sitting on the other side of the door from Misty."

"Whatever," he said and marched after Misty down the hall.

Margo watched him go, trying to get the image of Misty's bouncing breasts out of her mind. "How do you do this without losing your mind?" she asked Lynette.

"I just focus on the fact that I must remain sane to kill your brother and get away with it," the other woman said and prowled off down the hall.

Now, sitting in the lab with Jack, Misty, Chad, and Lynette, Margo had no trouble forgetting the Chad/Misty incident because three people had been on the rocket when it blew.

Her time on Mars wasn't fun anymore and she wanted off the planet. The whole trip had turned into a disaster. She wouldn't even get to test her rover, now that three deaths had occurred.

Lynette stared off into space looking shellshocked, sitting in the console chair and Margo wanted to join her. Out of the women who died, she had only really talked to one—Tiffany—who was an awesome person.

It's too bad Misty couldn't have been on the rocket instead.

Immediately after the thought, Margo felt horrible. She didn't mean that. Really she didn't. It was just the stress.

"All the clothing is gone, too," Lynette sobbed into a handkerchief Russ had produced from his pocket.

"What?" Jack asked, looking up from a cabinet he searched through.

"Our dresses are gone. We didn't move them," Margo said, staring at the screen, which showed the outside pile of dust.

"And the makeup and the interview room. We have nowhere to interview anyone," Lynette sniffed.

"Who cares?" Jack asked, pulling a large, rolled-up tube of paper from a stack.

Margo shook her head at him in warning. "She does. It's her job. She's having trouble adjusting to the show ending early."

"It isn't ending early," Lynette said. "The bachelor is still alive. The show must go on!"

"Lynette," Margo said gently, worried about the woman's mental health. "We can't keep filming. People died. That's totally disrespectful."

"We'll make it a tribute to Tiffany, Susan, and Rose."

Margo stared at her. "That's a terrible idea."

Lynette straightened. "They would want us to go on. They believed in Mars Bachelor."

Everyone stayed silent except Chad and Misty, who giggled as they sat on the floor on opposite sides of the door where Lynette had placed them until she figured out their punishment for breaking the rules. Misty slipped closer and ran her bare toe up and down Chad's leg. Chad blew her a kiss.

Three people just died and he voted her off. What is wrong with them? Margo turned away to see Jack unrolling a map onto a high table. "What are you doing?" she asked, looking for a distraction. Any distraction at all.

"I have a backup rover. On the off chance I can get it running again, I'm planning what I'll do next."

Margo drifted closer and saw it was a map of Mars.

He tapped the paper. "I bet whoever these people are, they haven't shut down the communications at Station 3."

"Why would they? Station 3 has been abandoned for almost a year."

He gave her a closer inspection. "You seem to be up on current events," he said, taking extra time to study her hiking boots.

"Margo," Lynette said, her tone a warning. Even in the middle of calamity, Lynette was still on the job.

"Yes, yes." Margo waved at her. She knew the rules, although it seemed dumb to follow them at this point. "I read up before I came," she told Jack.

He frowned as if that answer didn't satisfy him but turned back to the map. "I doubt I can fix my other rover. I have a parts problem."

"Actually we have one," she said, excitement bubbling up inside her. If Jack needed a rover, Lynette would have no choice but let Margo's out of hiding.

To drive her rover, to get out there and see the planet, to sense the rock beneath her feet, to experience the real terrain under her wheels. And on top of all that, they'd save everyone from a slow death. She would leave right now if she could.

"Margo," Lynette said again.

But Margo ignored her. "I brought a rover with me."

Boyle propped a hip against the table. "Is this one of those hallucinations some people have under extreme stress? Or an early case of Red Meningitis? Because we really don't have time for it."

Margo looked at the map. Could she make it to Station 3 without him? Because the thought of being alone with him made her shake inside. With anger, not with anything fun, despite the little zip of heat she'd experienced earlier. "I haven't been allowed to check the charge, but it should be close to full even with the slight loss during the downtime through space." All batteries shed energy when not in use. These might leak a little more, because they were attached to multiple solar panels, which allowed them to charge as it was driven.

Boyle peered at her closely, reached out a hand to check the temperature of her forehead. "Are you being serious?"

She ducked, not wanting to feel lust bolts again.

"As a heart attack." Estimating with her hand, she got a rough idea of how far away they were going. "130 miles is just on the edge of what my rover can do on its current battery with no downtime to recharge."

"What are you?" he asked, wondering how a woman with a rover had magically popped into his life right when he needed them.

"Mechanical engineer."

"Seriously?"

"Yes."

He shut up at that, trying to reconcile the beauty in the gold dress with the one standing before him.

"I want to see it," he said, clearly not buying that she had magically produced the answer to all his hopes.

She turned to Lynette, who shook her head. "You weren't allowed to test it until you were voted out. Hank was very insistent on that."

"Lynette, we might die here if we don't do something."

"And if we don't die, all of this is on film. It will get an Emmy at the very least. Maybe a Nobel Prize."

Jack snorted. "Prize for what? They don't give out Nobel Prizes for reality TV."

Lynette straightened, swiping at her tears. "Prize for filming the harrowing escape from Mars, at the very least."

Margo decided to ignore her. "She said she put it in one of the outbuildings."

"Let's go then." A slow smile spread across Boyle's face, making him look like a pirate in a movie film. A really hot pirate.

Wow. No wonder Jack Boyle never smiled. That smile was dangerous.

Lynette shouted something about contracts after Margo, but she didn't listen. This was it. This was her big moment, the thing she'd dreamed about her whole life. And she didn't care if her brother wouldn't pay her for being on the show. She was getting to drive at least 130 miles in her rover. On Mars.

"Space suits for this just in case the field fails," Boyle growled.

Normally inside the biodome, they didn't have to wear space suits, but the attack had weakened the field that held the air at tolerable standards. They would be glad they were in their suits if the field failed.

So, Boyle helped her get the fit right, giving her those same annoying shivers, then they stepped outside.

⌒‿⌒

Jack wondered if he was being punked. That was the only reasonable explanation he could come up with. Well, he guessed he'd see when they made it to the mechanical hut, which was the area he'd given to the film crew for their extra stuff. He'd checked it earlier, but hadn't looked in any of the crates.

Goldie walked beside him in her suit, her face full of what could only be described as joy. Jack had been joyous, too, when he'd first come here. But now this place had become a weight around his neck, pulling him down.

Her joy would fade soon, too, because he wasn't about to take her out with him.

He entered the mechanical hut, saw a large crate sitting in the center of the floor marked DO NOT OPEN. They unboxed it quickly and there before him was a shiny new rover. "What the hell," Jack whispered.

The mic in his helmet picked it up and Goldie bounded forward in the low gravity to place a hand on it. "She's a beauty, isn't she?"

Jack could only nod, because she was. Similar in structure to his old rover, this one had eight wheels with bigger tires but a smaller wheel base, the increased height allowing it to move around the massive and plentiful boulders and large rocks that made the ground a constant obstacle course, and allowed for tighter passage between them.

After a few moments of silence, he asked, "And you built this?"

"My team and I." She patted the rover with obvious pride.

"So, why the hell are you on this show?"

"I guess we're out of camera range." She peered all around, looking at the ceiling and checking an open bin. "So, I can tell you. I traded Hank filling in on the show for letting me test my rover here." She stretched her arms out wide, as if to say "tah dah!"

All of this annoyed him on many levels. First, Hank should have cleared this rover-testing business during their negotiations. He, Jack Boyle, should have had a say in any testing going on out of his station. Second, it was super annoying that her boyfriend sent her on this show to throw herself at another man, even if it was in the name of science. Not that Jack hadn't done a number of things he probably shouldn't for the same cause. Still, he couldn't shake his discomfort with the fact that this woman, this extraordinary woman, would be with an asshole like Hank Carson.

"I just don't understand why Hank would want his girlfriend vying for the opportunity to date another man," he said, disgusted.

She looked at him as if he was crazy. "Hank isn't my boyfriend. He's my brother."

"Brother? But your last name is Wilson."

"No, my last name is Carson. Margo Wilson is my code name for the show."

"Code name?"

"I think of it as my spy name."

"What?" he asked, totally confused.

"Never mind," she said. "I filled in for someone who broke her leg at the last minute. I was hoping to keep my career from being impacted, so I was using her name."

"Wait, your name isn't Margo either?"

"Well, actually it is, sort of. My brother calls me Margo. I bet that's why he thought of me to begin with," she said. "I wouldn't put it past him to have only thought of me because of the name thing, when I've spent my whole life wanting to get to Mars. My name is Margaret Carson. Although he stayed behind so I could test my rover on Mars, so I owe him."

"Not even your name is real. What the hell is the point of reality TV?" He shook his head, giving up because he needed her rover. "The issue remains that I didn't okay testing this," he said, hearing a snarl in his voice. He had once been asked by a lab assistant to stop snarling and occasionally he really did try not to.

The happiness fell off her face. "Well, you better be glad I brought her because she's going to save us."

"Give me a rundown on how to drive it."

She opened the door and leaned over, then jerked back. "Wait. You think you're taking her out alone, don't you?"

"Of course." He wasn't going to bring anyone else along. The Russians would blow him up the minute they saw him.

She folded her arms. "Not a chance. You won't be able to drive it without training, which I'm not giving to you. You have to take me."

"No one is coming with me. You have a better chance of staying alive here."

She put her hands on her hips, the gesture almost comical in the space suit. "I am testing this rover, period. No one, and I mean no one, goes anywhere in it without me in the driver's seat."

"We might get all the way to Station 3 and find the generator can't be restarted. No electricity means no com units. This whole thing could be a wild goose chase, one that will be dangerous. Because if Haxley is right, then it's only the buildings standing here that are keeping us alive right now. Whoever is out there can pick us off easily the minute we leave."

"I don't care. I drive or my rover stays in this shed."

He stared deep into her eyes and knew she meant it. He'd seen that same stubborn look in his own gaze too many times to think she'd waver.

For the first time in his life, he was in a corner. It made him seriously pissy. But what could he do? Even leaving first thing in the morning, it would take them a full day's journey to arrive at the other station. Then they'd have to get the communications equipment up and running, which might take hours or even longer depending on how the equipment had been left when the last team pulled out. Then return here the next morning, hopefully beating Hank Carson's shuttle's arrival, because it would have to leave without them if they didn't make it on time. The shuttle couldn't risk being destroyed as well. Turnaround speed would be critical to survival.

"I have waited my whole career for this moment, Boyle, and you're not taking this away from me."

"Okay, I'm taking you, but only under extreme protest."

"Your protest is noted," she said, a large smile blooming on her pretty lips.

He hoped he wasn't leading her into an early grave.

CHAPTER SEVEN

She was going to drive her rover on Mars. Margo let out a small squeal, because her current personality would totally squee in this moment.

They took a few hours to sleep, which was hard since a group date was being filmed nearby, the contestants playing board games with Chad. Although how the show would explain that they kept filming happy, fun group dates after people had died was beyond her, but clearly Lynette wasn't in her right mind. And everyone else was too narcissistic to give up on the possibility of fame or possibly too scared to lose their place on Paradise.

Putting her pillow over her head, Margo reflected that Monopoly always ended with hard feelings, no matter what planet you were on.

The next morning, she quickly packed an extra set of clothes, her second set of jeans, t-shirt and undies, into her smaller bag, adding the hidden stash of chocolate she'd brought, which had been expressly forbidden under the rules. The forms she'd signed had said she'd be searched when she boarded the rocket, but due to her late arrival, no one had gone through her things and her chocolate stash had been saved. No way she was leaving it behind. These girls were so stressed, they'd sniff it out the minute she left and that would be the end of it.

Amanda drifted over. "Going somewhere?" she asked, watching the packing process.

The other girls were in a huddle on the one sofa, crying and comforting each other as they reminisced about Tiffany, Susan, and Rose. They might not have known the dead women well, but they seemed genuinely upset by their deaths. Margo had to admit that as a group, they were all pretty nice. She spied Misty sitting alone on the other side of the room, and amended that most of them were nice.

"I'm helping Jack Boyle with a project." Margo figured she owed Amanda one for saving her from Misty's wrath.

"What's going on, Margo?" Amanda whispered. "You seem to know much more than you're telling."

Margo debated for a moment, then figured Hank could edit all this out and leaned close to whisper, "He thinks our rocket was destroyed by the Russians." She gave Amanda a nod when the other woman's eyes grew big. "And our communications with anyone off the planet has been cut. Jack and I are going to an old, closed station to try to get a message out."

"But why you?" Amanda asked. "What's the deal with you? No offense, but you haven't fit in since the beginning."

So much for Margo thinking these women were stupid. Nothing got by them. "I'm not allowed to tell. Lynette would have my head if I did."

Amanda seemed to believe her and didn't push, asking instead, "Are we in trouble here?"

"Maybe." Margo put her hand on Amanda's shoulder. "Keep them calm. You're a leader and they need leadership." Then she threw her bag over her shoulder and left the room quickly, as if she knew what she was doing.

Which she did not.

The fact was, while she had tested her rover, no sequence of scenarios could conclusively prove that the vehicle was ready for the real world. Well, the real world of Mars, that is. There came a point when she just had to bring it to Mars and drive it. This was that point, but that didn't mean she wasn't worried.

The trip to Station 3 wasn't an optimal testing environment either. If something went wrong when they were a hundred miles away, no one could come get them. They would be on their own and she didn't have all her equipment with her to fix certain things if they went wrong, although she'd stowed away a decent repair kit. When she'd made the deal with Hank, she'd envisioned driving around the biodome for a few hours, then tinkering to make minor adjustments. Then driving around the biodome again. Not an emergency dash to another station.

She and Boyle spent time loading supplies, jamming them into the crevasses in the rover. She realized a little more storage space would be optimal, if she could work it out.

When the rising sun blasted across the expanse in front of the station, they headed out.

They started with the sun at their backs, then turned west. Boyle had been monosyllabic since they'd left, so Margaret decided to concentrate on the rover. And she was Margaret now, because there was no reason to be Margo. No camera had been installed, despite Lynette's best attempt to get one placed. Boyle had put the kibosh on that immediately, telling her every bit of space had to go to the current mission.

He'd called it that, a mission, and his demeanor showed he believed it. The way he was acting, he definitely had military in his background.

Margaret had decided to forget about the Russians or the Chinese or maybe aliens for all she knew, and concentrate on having the experience of her lifetime.

The terrain was what she'd expected and planned for, but the very air on Mars seemed to put an odd strain on the engine that the simulation chamber hadn't anticipated.

She weaved through large boulders, the tires easily churning through the small pea gravel and rocks below. The GPS screen on the dash showed her where to go, so they didn't have to talk. She wondered if he was always so silent, or if he was still annoyed she'd forced him to let her go.

The engine skipped a beat, just a quick hesitation that reverberated in her arms.

She hit the brakes.

"What the hell?" Boyle asked, grabbing the dash.

"Close up your suit. I need to check something." She turned and reached over to the small back seat where she'd stashed a couple of tools.

"We've barely made it past the Station boundaries. You telling me this thing is already failing?"

"It hasn't failed. I'm making a minor adjustment." A protective instinct welled up, making her snappish. How dare he insult her rover? Of course it hadn't failed.

She put on her gloves and helmet, closing her suit flaps. Then she mimed pulling the top open, threatening him with exposure to the surface if he didn't put his gear on.

He did, muttering something she didn't catch and giving her a grumpy look.

She got out, and annoyingly he followed her. Releasing the engine compartment cover, she leaned in. He cut off her light by leaning in with her. She turned her head inside the helmet, which was locked in a forward position, and glared at him. His helmet almost kissed her own. She banged her wrench on his head to get his attention, making him jump. Then they were staring eye to eye, so close that if they weren't suited up, she would have pulled back from the intimacy of it all.

"You're blocking my light," she said, louder than necessary, but what the hell did he think he was going to do here? Because he surely wasn't touching her engine.

He jerked a little, then stepped back. "Sorry," he said, and actually sounded it.

She returned to the engine, tightening the choke a half turn. She closed the cover.

"That was it?"

"We could have driven on with it the way it was, but it would drain the batteries and we can't afford that."

He climbed back into the rover.

She started the engine again and smiled at the perfect purr.

The sun had risen and the ground turned from a dark red to more of a reddish brown, with big rocks and boulders filling the landscape. It was a surreal vista that inspired nothing short of complete awe in Margaret. A shiver ran up her spine.

"You okay?" Jack asked, seemly attuned to her emotions.

"Yes," she said, suddenly self-conscious. "Just a bit awestruck that I'm actually here."

"Even though you had to play a brain-dead bimbo to get here? You don't seem ashamed of being on the show. I think I would be."

She raised an eyebrow at that, offended at first, but she quickly reminded herself that was exactly what she thought of the show and its contestants too. She gave him the truth. "It turns out I'd sell my soul to the devil to get to Mars."

They were silent after that for a long time. Then Jack said, "I guess I did, too, when it comes down to it."

"Did what?"

"Sold my soul to the devil to live on Mars."

"How?"

"I needed money so badly I let Hank Carson take over my station."

"I wouldn't be too hard on yourself. Hank can get most people to do what he wants." She remembered when Hank had gotten her to "invest" months of her allowance in a new comic book he wrote in middle school. He'd managed to pay back part of her money before he'd had to fold when the principal told him to stop selling the comics or she'd kick him out of the private school their parents scraped and saved to send them to.

"Your brother is on my shit list."

"He's on mine, too. But don't go overboard running him down. He's still my brother, the only one I've got, and I'll throw you out of my rover to walk back if you get too nasty about him."

"Message received," he said, dryly.

She smiled at his tone. They were coming to an understanding. She found she might like Jack Boyle after all.

CHAPTER EIGHT

*J*ack sat in the passenger seat, watching the woman he now knew was Margaret Carson drive. Her name seemed vaguely familiar. If she really built rovers, that might be why.

It was both lucky and odd to have her on the planet. Her rover totally changed everything. Their only hope of warning the resupply rocket was to send a communication. Otherwise, whoever was bombing them would end up simply taking the resupply rocket out and there weren't a lot of options left to get off the planet. Rockets weren't exactly thick on the ground on Earth.

Jack had known moving to Mars might end in his death. If anything went wrong with his health, for example, he would have to wait until the supply rocket came to return him to Earth. Station 5 also had a supply stream, so in theory, they would act as each other's back up, but Jack hated Haxley so much, he'd always thought he'd die before asking for help.

Although when it came down to it, he had called Haxley. That was something to think on. Of course, it was easier to call when other people's lives were at stake.

Now they were in a serious jam and he couldn't just pick up the phone to dial 911.

This whole journey was a long shot. All his hopes were pinned on Station 3's equipment being in usable condition. He'd tried to warn Margaret that this might be a one-way ticket, but she hadn't listened. But he knew. If they got there and they were missing anything essential to get the generator up and running, then they had no choice but to go back and hope for the best, having risked everything for nothing. On top of it all, both directions they'd be sitting ducks, waiting to be blown to bits.

As they drove, he considered if he had it in him to stay on Mars for another quarter. Assuming he lived, of course. Running the station was a burden he hadn't been prepared for. Not the loneliness, he was okay with that. But all the work begging for money, when he just wanted to stare at rocks and learn their secrets.

Margaret drove well, working them around the large boulders and occasional drop offs that seemed to appear out of nowhere. The terrain was choppy and he'd always chafed under the slow driving conditions, but she had endless patience.

They stopped around midday to let the batteries charge a bit in the sun while they grabbed something to eat and stretched their legs. Margaret looked under the hood again and he stood aside, finding that somewhere along the way, he'd decided he trusted her. After all, it was her rover and her life was in as much danger as his.

If he was honest, he'd admit he was attracted to her, especially now that she'd changed out of the gold dress and into clothes he felt more comfortable with. And the fact she was a scientist didn't hurt either. Perhaps it was just that he hadn't been around a woman in a long, long time, but he didn't think so. He could tell Goldie and he had an attraction on a basic level.

They were roughly halfway to Station 3 and he was confident now that they'd make it before sunset. Driving across this terrain was impossible in the dark due to bitingly low temperatures and harsh winds. The one time he'd been caught out, he'd been lucky to make it back and had never pushed close to sunset again.

He ate a quick lunch and wandered over to investigate a small cave formation. It was bigger than he'd thought. Seeing something glittering in the back of the cave, he carefully inched in and crouch-walked to the shiny object. Taking his flashlight off his belt, he lit up the wall. It twinkled as the beam hit, creating a small rainbow.

Could it be diamonds?

Surely not.

And yet, the facets rainbowed in his flashlight like diamonds would.

But only cut and polished diamonds made a rainbow and these were raw. His gut said they were something else entirely, because Mars didn't have the base materials to make diamonds.

Excitement zipped through him. This could be the discovery that was the crowning achievement of his career.

Static interrupted his study. He ignored it, but when it came again, he realized Goldie was trying to reach him.

He went to the cave's entrance and hit his com button. "You calling me?"

"Yeah, something flew overhead."

"Is it still out there?"

"I don't see it anymore."

Jack's first instinct was to run to her, but he stood still just outside the cave. "Keep low and come to me. I'm northwest of you."

"On my way."

"As fast as you can move without falling."

If the Russians dropped ordinance on the rover, he didn't want her killed. Although, hell, they didn't have enough oxygen to get back to Station 7 or forward to Station 3. So, they were dead either way.

"I can see you," he said as she rounded a rock, a wrench still in her hand.

She moved well, her body working with the lack of gravity instead of against it, bounding in a forward leaping stance like a pro. It was clear she'd been in a gravity tank before. No one started out this good.

"Come on," he said, and grabbed her arm as she neared to help her stop.

They ducked into the cave.

For a few minutes, they stood waiting, both frozen in place. Listening, holding their breath.

Nothing happened. Minutes ticked by.

Unable to help it, Jack moved to the back of the cave again and studied the formation. He didn't have any of his collection tools, but he needed a sample. "Let me have your wrench."

"Why?" she asked, coming up beside him. "Wait, are those diamonds?"

"I think they're a new type of quartz." He ran a finger along the face of a larger specimen, wishing he could take it into the light.

"Are you going to knock my wrench against those rocks?" she asked suspiciously.

"Yes."

She stepped back, holding the tool close to her chest. "Do you know how much these cost? They're a titanium alloy mix."

He held out his hand. "I need a sample," he insisted. Because he did. If these were diamonds, just sitting here, and if he made it out of this mess alive, then this could be the answer to all his money questions. Two rather big ifs at the moment. And if it wasn't diamonds, which was more likely, then it might be something totally new. The thought excited him more than the answer to all his cash flow issues. Which was why he should never have signed up to run a station alone.

She still cradled the wrench against her, obviously not wanting to give it to him.

"I'll let you drive all the way back from Station 3 tomorrow," he said, part of him doubting they would be around for tomorrow. The other part of him thought they were going to get out of this in one piece, he was going to have discovered a new type of quartz on Mars, and his whole life was about to change.

"I was already driving back."

He closed and opened his hand. "This is important."

She paused a beat, but placed it on his palm.

He freed a few shards with several hard smacks. She hissed as if he'd hurt her.

Handing the tool back, he gathered the pieces. Straightening, he noticed her examining the handle in the dim light by the edge of the cave.

"It's a wrench," he reminded her.

She gave him an insulted frown. "It's not just any wrench, just like those rocks aren't just any rocks."

She had a point, so he gave her a small nod.

"Daylight is burning," she said, peering out of the cave at the sky.

"I agree." The heavens were empty. "Do we stay or go?" He didn't like waiting around for them to come back and blow up the rover. Maybe it was a small chance, but he'd rather make a run for Station 3 then stay here.

"Go," she said, without hesitation.

"I agree. Let's get out of here."

They moved quickly, without further discussion, and climbed into the vehicle.

She had it in gear and going before he'd even put on his seatbelt.

Despite not stopping again, they made slow time.

"You need me to spell you?" he asked.

"Not a chance."

"Wow, and I thought I was controlling," he teased, but he liked her moxie.

"Huh," she said, then fell silent working them around a tricky piece of ground.

It took thirteen hours, but they rolled into Station 3 with an hour's daylight to spare. Margaret slowed as they crested the hill so they could take a long look. Everything seemed abandoned and quiet.

"Well I guess the Russians aren't using this as a base," she said.

"No."

"It looks like it's been abandoned for years instead of less than one."

She was right. The fine, red dust that covered everything on Mars had drifted in once the biodome field stopped sheltering the space. The winds and storms had beaten all the buildings into a weathered, falling-down ramshackle of a sad little village.

They rolled forward, parking the rover inside a small lean-to to keep it away from prying eyes. He hoped the winds would pick up to cover their tracks.

Then they went into the largest building, figuring that would hold all the equipment.

Station 3 had been a working research center for less than two years. The staff hadn't been able to keep their testing equipment running after several storms came through and caused energy surges. The cost of upkeep far outpaced the money the United States government was willing to shell out. Congress voted to shut the station down and the researchers living here, all of whom were suffering from either a flu-like illness or Red Meningitis or both, were flown out and the station temporarily shut down. Congress never approved a NASA budget big enough to open it again. When the US government had gotten out of the Mars exploration business, others had stepped in to fill the gap, and private ventures like Jack's had sprung up.

What Jack counted on was the fact that it was supposed to be a temporary decampment. Which meant they'd left everything in place. He hoped.

All the buildings were constructed out of prefabricated metal and wood from Earth. Due to the cost of rocket fuel, everything had been abandoned when they left. Just as his station would be deserted when he returned to Earth. Which could be on the next quarterly shuttle, the way things were going.

That's if he lived long enough to get on the quarterly shuttle.

The building they entered was a combination command center and living quarters. The left half of the room held the same console setup as his lab. The right was a small sitting area with a sofa and two chairs, a small dining table and what looked like a galley kitchen. A door led to the back of the building, probably to sleeping areas and storage. Dust lay thick and undisturbed on the floor.

He shut the door behind them, kicking up a cloud which obscured his view for a moment before it settled again.

He waved a hand in front of his face to clear the air. "All of this is garbage. Even on a different planet, Americans manage to litter."

Goldie picked up an abandoned coffee mug still sitting on the kitchen table. "Well, we're glad they left all this stuff, or we wouldn't have a hope of calling home."

"We still might not." He surveyed the equipment in the far left corner, staring at the stacks of abandoned binders and notebooks, wondering what they contained that had been so disposable, they could leave them behind. "There is no reason the console wouldn't work. As far as they knew, they were returning or another crew was taking their place on the next rocket up here," he said, trying to reassure them both.

"Only one way to find out. Fire up the generator and see."

"It will be in one of the outbuildings, in case of fire." In fact, there should be two, since without a generator, they would die without a steady supply of oxygen.

"Let's go find it, then."

They trooped back and split up to search the five small buildings. The first building held a rover, the wheels flat to the ground, covered in dust.

Static came in his ears and he figured she was calling him. He stepped outside. "Goldie?" he asked.

She leaned out of a nearby hut and waved him over. "What's up with the Goldie name anyway?"

"From the dress you were wearing when I met you," he said, squatting down to look at the weathered generator. It had taken a beating. Rust already browned the edges and most of the paint had been stripped away by the wind coming in from the missing boards on the far wall.

He flipped on the switch. Nothing happened.

"You have to prime it," she said.

"I keep forgetting I have a mechanic with me."

"I'm hardly a mechanic," she said, her tone prim and annoyed.

He grinned.

"It'll take a bit for me to figure it out," she said, clearly implying she wanted him to go elsewhere.

He stood, relieved to gift her the task. "All yours. I'm going to have a look around, unless you think you'll need me?"

"I'd rather you not stand over me," she said, her voice a bit distracted and a bit commanding.

Normally he didn't take orders from others, but he discovered he liked her tendency to boss him around.

"I'm gone then," he said.

She didn't react, already having forgotten him as she leaned closer to the generator and opened a panel he hadn't even known was there.

Thank God he'd brought her. He would have been screwed trying to get it started. The thought he might have to fix the generator hadn't even crossed his mind, although it should have. That showed how rattled he'd been when the rocket had blown.

He went back to the main building. The coffee mug Goldie had touched earlier still sat on the table, a stack of papers beside it. As if someone had stood up and walked away. Creepy. Like some sort of Stephen King movie.

The people who'd once been here had all lived. He'd met the mission leader before he'd left Earth, so he knew for a fact they were alive and well.

But part of him thought the scene before him had come from the Walking Dead.

He forced himself to study the control panel, making sure it was still intact.

Beside him, a floor lamp jumped to life, making him start.

"Okay, enough of that," he said firmly. No more jumping at shadows or comparing his surroundings to horror movies.

"Enough of what?" Goldie asked, shutting the door they'd left standing open.

"This place is creeping me out."

She studied the control panel, looking for the on switch he'd bet.

He walked to the left side and threw the switch.

"Oh, it's there."

"Same panel as at Station 7," he said. There hadn't been anyone else to buy from, not that he would have. He hadn't been able to afford upgrades.

The computer went through its boot cycle and he brought over a straight-backed chair from the table for her to sit in, then took the one at the console.

"Wow, that was gentlemanly of you to bring me a chair," she murmured.

"It's just a chair," he said, distracted as they stared at the cursor as it blinked and numbers flashed by, taking its time as it thought whatever computers thought when they'd been neglected for so long.

Finally, it ended by asking for a password.

"Damn," he said, his heart sinking. He didn't have a password on his computer. Why would he? It wasn't like some stranger was going to come in off the street and get his personal information. Station 3 had had more people, but they were all on the same team. They shouldn't need passwords from each other.

"Do you know the password?" she asked.

"Nope."

"Oh shit," she said.

"Yeah," he agreed.

CHAPTER NINE

"We are royally screwed," Boyle said, pacing around the room, still trying to come up with passwords.

They'd tried everything he could think of—combinations of the team name and the year, famous rover names, and last names of the team members themselves. She'd contributed "password" and "Mars" with the date Station 3 had become operational. But none of them had worked and really it could be anything.

"At least they don't have a password limit set up, or we'd have been locked out a hundred tries ago," she said, trying to look on the bright side.

He grunted, but kept pacing.

Jack Boyle was an interesting guy, part scientist, part explorer, part warrior. She felt comfortable with him, even though they'd had a rough start.

"We could eat," she suggested, realizing she was hungry.

"We can only stay here through the morning, tops, before we have to leave. If we miss the shuttle, we're stuck here until we starve to death." Boyle went through the stack of paper on the console, flipping pages aggressively. Then he put his hands on his hips and sighed. "But we aren't accomplishing anything right now, so let's eat."

"I'll get the pack," she said, starving now all of a sudden. She slipped outside quickly to release as little of the increasing pressure inside the main building as possible. Once it had risen to Earth's oxygen level, they'd be able to take off their suits. She trudged across the space, feeling the drive catch up with her. She was pretty damn tired. Perhaps she should lie down and sleep after grabbing a quick bite.

The sun was setting and for a moment she watched it in awe, then she scanned the sky for the Russians. Nothing greeted her except red golden rays bathing the broken landscape.

Then it hit her. She'd be spending the night alone with Jack Boyle. The thought made her shiver.

⌒

Jack stared at the password prompt, hearing Goldie come back in behind him.

He wondered if this was it, if they'd come all this way, only to be met with such a simple roadblock.

Fabric crinkled and rustled behind him. "I think the oxygen level is high enough now to take off our suits."

From out of nowhere, he suddenly wished he'd had a more normal life. With a wife. And kids, maybe. A home filled with pretty rocks and sunlight that wasn't red except at the end of a glorious day. He'd never wanted these things before, but now faced with his own mortality, he found he did.

For all that he'd wanted to be on Mars, he didn't want to die here.

"I'm going to see if their cleaning unit is still up and running and try to get some of the spacesuit ick off me."

He should do that too. He knew time in a suit made him smell atrocious. It usually didn't matter but he found he didn't want Goldie smelling him that way.

He typed in a series of his favorite old school astronauts—Armstrong, Aldrin, Gene Cernan who did the longest moon walk ever at twenty-two hours. The list went on and on.

"We should eat," she said, resting a hand on his shoulder, the touch adding to the strange melancholy that had swamped him. "This seems harder than it really is because we're hungry." The gesture was oddly comforting, though. And it occurred to him he'd been waiting for someone to touch him just like that his whole life. He wanted to turn and capture her hand, pull her close for a hug. Or more.

He tapped his finger on his leg, trying to focus on the password again, but he knew they needed to shake it up and stop doing the same things over and over, getting the same results. "You're right. We'd planned to spend the night here anyway and it will be dark soon." He stepped out of his suit. "The cleaning unit still work?"

"Yep, seemed to."

"I'll go take my turn in it. Be right back." His last glance over his shoulder showed her unpacking their meager provisions. He found the sight strangely comforting.

When he returned, she had meal kits warming on the now working stove. He helped her set the table, then they sat down and ate in an awkward silence. He tried to come up with something to talk about but had no interest in rehashing their impending deaths and didn't think any other subject would come across as normal.

"It feels nice to be out of the suits," she said.

"Yeah," he said, feeling stupid. Why was he struggling to talk to this woman? He'd had no problem until she touched him and brought up all sorts of weird emotions. He'd never wanted to live like a civilian before.

"I'm trying to come up with a topic that doesn't include Russians or death," she said.

He sputtered a laugh, realizing that they were similar thinkers. "Yeah. I'm sick of thinking about that too. Russians and death are off limits for the duration."

They lapsed back into silence, but the tension had eased, with nothing below the surface. It was the same silence he had at mealtime most nights, only better because he had a gorgeous sexy scientist across from him.

"Did you get an endowment for Station 7?" she asked.

"Nope. I did the whole thing with grants." It had been a complete bitch.

"Wow. How many did it take?" From her voice, she understood completely the enormity of what he'd done.

"Fourteen."

Her mouth dropped open. "So many. How many from the government?"

"Six." He watched the horror grow on her face. This was a woman who had done her share of government grants.

"Oh my God. The work must have been crushing."

With the amount of documentation required, government grants tore your soul from your body.

He nodded. "Total hell, and I'm almost out of money again."

"You didn't go the sponsor route?"

"Maybe I made a mistake there, but I didn't want some battery company using me as a spokesman and making this into a money machine for them." Not that he hadn't had a ton of offers. Sports cars and watch companies, health insurance and video games, they'd all wanted a piece of him. He regretted now that he hadn't taken the easy money.

"Changing your mind now?" she asked.

"I'm leaning in that direction."

"I would have broken long ago. You must be one stubborn person not to fold under that pressure."

"This reality TV thing was my first step into selling out."

She shook her head. "You aren't selling out. Compromises have to be made to get things accomplished. That's just life. Mars is worth some sacrifices."

"Mars is worth everything." He met her gaze and they shared a moment of complete accord. He was pretty sure no one understood exactly what he'd given up—and gained—when it came to Mars. Except maybe this woman.

Seemingly caught up in this moment of realization herself, she cleared her throat to break the silence and intensity of their shared experience. "For me too, obviously. You might have to put up with us for a month, but I had to squeeze into a ball gown and accept a rose from some a-hole who only kept me around to get back at Lynette."

"Who's Lynette? The women who's running things?" he guessed, realizing that he hadn't been properly introduced earlier.

"Yeah. Don't underestimate her. She might have had a small breakdown after those people died, but she's a ballbuster at heart."

"You sound like you like her."

"I do. She's got the toughest job on the planet I think."

"Huh." Not that his job was hard, not the geologist part anyway. He'd always found his work a joy. "Did you have a sponsor for the rover? Or did the university support you?" He took the last bite of his meal.

"Are you kidding? We're a public university. Funding is nonexistent. And I haven't found a sponsor who is even remotely excited about a climbing rover. But NASA paid a large chunk with the understanding I'd share my design."

"Ouch." That meant NASA would not need to buy rovers from her in the future. They could make their own, cutting out her ability to sell her design to a manufacturer and make a large amount of money.

"Not really. The knowledge I'll gain is going to set my research so far ahead, they'll struggle to catch up when I give it to them. I made my delivery date much further out than I needed to."

"I'm surprised they let you."

"They didn't have a choice. I know my worth."

It was nice, really, to talk to someone who understood what his world was like. They finished their meal and recycled their meal packs, then the hunt was on again for the password. It had to be here somewhere and with food in their bellies, they were focused and on top of their game.

Jack wasn't a person to give up, but time was running out and he needed to get into the computer. It was already dark outside, the atmosphere through the portholes fading to the dusky red that signaled the end of the day. Too bad he wasn't some sort of hacker. But computers had never held the allure like rocks had.

Goldie sat nearby, going through a stack of what looked like daily logbooks that were handwritten. Which was odd. He would have thought they would either be computerized or taken back to Earth when the team left. Perhaps they'd been too ill to pack properly.

Margaret Carson was an interesting woman, one he hoped to get to know better. What he liked most was that she understood the trials of his world and she respected his research. She didn't question why he would be on Mars. Sure, it sounded sexy at first, but the reality was, he was camping out here, living a rustic existence, and he would live like this for as long as he could. Mars had always been his first priority and no significant other would come first. He'd never met a woman before who understood his devotion to the red planet.

Until now.

Margaret had made her own sacrifices. Six months ago, he would have looked down on her for them, but now he understood. Hell, he'd jumped on the chance to have Hank Carson film at Station 7.

The more he thought of it, the more he admired her for taking the opportunity to come, even if it meant she had to be on a reality TV show.

As he stared at her, an odd thought filtered through his mind. What if he wasn't alone at Station 7? What if someone else was there with him? Someone doing their own experiments? Someone like Margaret Carson?

Thoughts of what it would be like to have another person in his living space didn't repel him as they usually did. In fact, they were… pleasant.

"What about this?" Margaret asked, pointing at a page in the journal.

He leaned down close to her to look. She smelled like machine oil, Mars dust, and vaguely like herbal shampoo. He wanted to move closer for a deeper sniff.

"There," she said, pointing to the top corner, where Spac3junky3! was written.

"Looks like a password for sure." Feeling oddly reluctant to stop sniffing her, he went to the console. "You have the honors," he said, holding out a chair.

She sat, letting him roll her a bit closer. Then she typed it in.

They waited, wondering if it would work.

The monitor flashed off, then on again, and for a second he thought they'd blown it, but then it read, WELCOME TO STATION 3.

"We're in," she cried, victorious, leaping to her feet.

He grabbed her arm and swung her to his chest, planting a kiss on her lips. It was closed mouthed and chaste, but he felt the shiver of need for the first time in so very, very long.

He knew she felt it too, as her arms threaded around his neck, their kiss deepening as her lips parted.

CHAPTER TEN

*A*nd then the computer beeped.

They sprung apart, and she said, "We're in." A pretty blush rose across her cheeks.

"Yeah," he said, trying to remember what they were doing. The simple kiss had thrown him for a loop. Maybe he was getting old. When he was younger, he wouldn't have been so flustered. But now pressing his lips to another person's had him flummoxed on a deep level. Because all he could think was that he wanted to kiss her again, keep on kissing her for a long time, forgetting all their troubles and worries.

So he did.

He framed her face in his hands and traced the seam of her lips with his tongue. She caught her breath in a gasp, putting her hands on top of his. But not to pull them away.

After a long moment, he rested his forehead on hers, trying to catch his breath. Kissing Goldie might be better than sex.

But not sex with her, a little voice said inside his head. He'd bet sex with her would be amazing.

"Russians," he said, to remind himself.

"Right," she said, breathless.

He focused on the Russians and warning the shuttle, reluctantly stepping away to take the seat she'd vacated. She dragged over the kitchen chair he'd given her earlier.

It was a simple process to send messages out. The program already had most of the people he wanted to contact in the address book. He retyped the same message he'd composed before and hit send. Then they stared at it, side by side, silent. She grasped his hand and he clasped hers back, enjoying the touch. For a long time, they stayed that way, waiting for it to error like the last one had.

"Nothing," she said, breaking the silence.

Reluctantly, he dropped her hand to click to the outbox, making sure it wasn't still there, his brain slow and sluggish as he tried to think about their situation and not how much he might like her. He couldn't believe he had what amounted to an infatuation building inside him, his whole body tingling with a need he hadn't known was possible.

"It looks like it sent," he agreed. He clicked around a few more times, refreshing, before he gave in to the hope that he'd gotten the message out.

"Should we call Station 7? Let them know?"

"Good idea," he said, glad she, at least, was thinking of something besides their kiss. And sex. He tapped around, a little lost in the new system, which was almost, but not quite, like his own.

Then he located the coms application and stared at it for a few moments, wondering how to reach his station, which hadn't been in operation when this station was running and therefore hadn't had a channel already set up between them. He tried to remember how he'd set up the com to Haxley.

He pondered for long, agonizing seconds, then managed to reach out to someone. If it turned out to be Haxley, who was hopefully still alive, he'd have the older man patch him through.

But instead of Haxley, Russ' face filled the screen. "Whoa, wasn't expecting to see you two," the cameraman said, his voice filled with relief.

"Everything okay there?" Margaret asked.

"Well, Lynette had them go on individual dates today and is now doing a cocktail party and rose ceremony."

"You're kidding," Jack said before he thought better of it. But come on! They were in the middle of an emergency here.

Russ shrugged. "It's kept everyone calm and under control."

"That's a good idea, actually," Margaret said.

"She is totally miffed you aren't here, Margo. She said when you get back, she's making you do extra shots so they can slide you in digitally."

Margaret shrugged off the punishment. "Okay."

Her easy capitulation had Jack shaking his head, but he'd spent what? An hour debating letting them film at the station? "We were able to send out warnings," Jack said, bringing them back to the important stuff, like how they were going to survive.

"Awesome," Russ fist pumped the air. "I knew you'd do it, Boyle."

Jack was oddly pleased at the compliment. "Yeah, well we've done all we can. We'll get some sleep, then leave for Station 7 at first light. Remember, if we don't make it back for some reason, you must get everyone on the shuttle and out of here as fast as you can. You can't wait for us."

Russ' face fell. "That doesn't seem right."

"Whoever's blowing up our vehicles will kill you too if you aren't out of here as fast as possible. Promise me you'll make that happen."

Russ shook his head, but said, "I promise. Well, if I don't see you, good luck."

"You too," Jack said, signing off.

They'd done what they could. He and Margaret sat staring at the blank console screen.

"I wish we could start back. Missing the shuttle sounds pretty ominous."

"Sadly, we can't travel in the dark." He stood. "We should sleep while we can." It had been a long day. But he really didn't want to sleep. He wanted to kiss her again. Maybe do more than kissing. He stomped down on his imagination as it conjured what else they could do.

She glanced to a viewport. "How long until morning?"

Mars' rotation was slightly less than an hour longer than Earth's. "Eight hours at least, maybe a little more." He wouldn't kiss her, though, because they both needed sleep. "They had six people living here. There should be multiple beds to choose from in the back of the building. Maybe we could each get our own space," he said, secretly hoping he was wrong.

Because he didn't want to have his own space. He wanted to strip off her clothes and run his tongue along all that pretty skin of hers.

Where had that come from? He wasn't the kind of guy who ran around lusting. Or maybe he hadn't been, but he was now that he'd met Goldie.

Or maybe this was the beginning of Red Meningitis. The first sign was altered mental status. Like doing things that were clearly not in the person's best interest. For example, having an affair with a contestant from the Mars Bachelor.

They located the bedroom quickly, since besides the bath and what had obviously been a lab, it was the only other room in the building. Three sets of bunk beds, slightly smaller than the ones he and his brother had shared as kids, filled the room, along with six small dressers.

The walls were covered with pictures from home. Goldie stepped near to study one group still taped to the wall behind the closest bunk. "They all lived, right?"

"Yeah." He leaned on the doorframe, oddly reluctant to enter the room.

"Why does it feel like they all died horrible deaths?"

"I don't know, but it does." He didn't want to sleep here, he realized. Wouldn't sleep here, with all those family members staring down at him.

"They got some sort of sickness, didn't they?"

"Red Meningitis. It's a bacterial infection."

"Did they all get it?"

"No. Only a few of them. The doctors think it affects only twenty percent of space travelers, but three of them had it. They all lived, though," he added, trying to console them both.

She looked up. "I don't want to stay in here."

Relief flooded through him. "Me either."

She let out a breath. "What other options do we have?" she asked, passing him as she hustled out the door.

They returned to the main room and studied the two overstuffed chairs and the sofa, which looked ancient, but he knew it was most likely less than three years old. "You take the couch and I'll push these chairs together and sleep there."

"I should take the chairs. You're bigger than I am."

"We're close to the same height," he said, realizing it was true. She must be somewhere around five-ten. "You'll be more comfortable on the couch."

"You're being awfully nice to me, Jack Boyle," she said, digging in one of their packs for a couple of thin blankets.

He took one and gave her a roguish grin. "Maybe because I like you," he said, wincing in surprise at his own words.

She raised her eyebrows. "Wow."

"Don't let it go to your head."

"I'll try not to." She stared at the sofa. "Does this lay flat?"

He realized they'd brought the flimsy furniture here to save weight and the back did, indeed, lower down flat. "I think you're right."

She flipped a hidden lever on her side and suddenly they had a bed. "Sleep here together?"

It would be more comfortable than the chair by miles, although he wondered how much sleep he'd get so close to her. Fuck it. "I'm game."

While she used the bathroom, he rearranged the throw pillows a couple times unnecessarily. Then caught himself and stopped. But it had been a long day.

When he returned from the bathroom, she was already lying down on one edge.

He took his assigned spot, fighting the urge to slide in next to her instead. And they lay there silently for a moment, neither sleeping.

"I'm exhausted but can't sleep," she murmured.

"Me either." He couldn't sleep because she was right beside him and he wanted to run his hands all over her and maybe follow that with his mouth. "Where did you go to school?" he asked, grasping for something to talk about.

She answered with relief, laughing as he made fun of their mascot and questioning their geology department, as if that mattered to anyone who wasn't a geologist.

They talked about everything and nothing for a long time, comparing their experiences, from grad school nightmares, research woes, and the constant pressure of remaining relevant in the scientific community, to family, friends, and everything in between. He liked the sound of her voice, liked how interested she was in his work and how he found what she did fascinating. Laughing at some old story he told, she rolled toward him and his pulse quickened.

Down boy, he told his libido. "You shouldn't get too close to me. I won't be held responsible for my actions if you cross into my zone," he warned, his voice suddenly rough with desire, but deadly serious.

Without warning, she climbed on top of him, pressing her stomach against his full erection, which he'd been trying to ignore. "You like me, hmm?" she asked, her voice a purr.

Of course now he couldn't ignore it with her body weight pressing into him.

"Looks like I'm not the only one in the mood," she whispered, the words husky in the darkness, only the computer screen still blinking in the far left corner for light.

"I didn't want to presume."

"When we get back to Station 7, best case scenario is that we have an audience. Worst case, we die." She ran a hand down his chest. "I really think we should take this moment while we can."

He kissed her, not having to think twice. The need that he'd been trying so hard to keep in check exploded over him, and he entwined his legs with hers.

She struggled back and he released her immediately. "Whoa, whoa there cowboy. We have some terms to set first."

"Terms?" he asked, trying to call his brain back from wherever it had gone.

"We can't have sex."

"We can't?" he asked, knowing he sounded like an idiot, but really his brain had flipped off completely the moment she'd climbed on top of him.

"Not unless you have a condom?" she asked hopefully.

His libido deflated, but sadly not enough. "No."

"I figured. Then we're going to have to get creative about this."

His excitement level climbed back up again. "Yeah?"

"Are you open to that?"

"I am," he agreed, so quickly she laughed, a deep throat, sexy laugh that had him kissing her again.

He'd never been big on intimate sexual conversations, but he stroked her pulse point with one finger while she laid out her plan. Anything that didn't involve penetration was fair game. She was open to any of his wildest fantasies, but he hoped he wouldn't disappoint her, since adventure wasn't in his most wanted sex list. It had been so long, what he really needed was to come, and since it wouldn't be inside her, it would have to be some other way, preferably with her coming too at the same time.

Slowly, trying to make it as good for her as it was for him, he ran his hands along her body, helping lift off her shirt. He rolled her under him and skimmed her jeans free, leaving her socks on, since it was chilly inside the living space, despite the chugging sound of the heater they'd turned on.

She reached for the button on his pants, but he blocked her hand. "Best to keep things battened down so we don't have any mistakes."

"Good idea." She laughed again, the sound so sexual, he shivered in response.

Then he kissed her, inching along her beautiful body, until he could suck gently on a nipple as she arched below him.

Slow down, he advised himself. He licked from her stomach to her hip, biting gently along the edge. He spent some time there, pressing his palm onto the apex of her thighs, loving the twist of her body as she squirmed closer.

"God," she whispered. "I want you so badly."

He hummed into her flesh, loving her in that moment.

Then he parted the lips of her sex and ran his tongue along her, enjoying her taste and smell, reveling in the fact that he was so lucky, way out on Mars, to have this beautiful woman below him.

He set a pace, working her to climax, keeping things light and slow until her hand twisted in his hair and she demanded, "Faster."

He obliged, working as hard as he'd ever worked in his life, because nothing had ever meant so much to him than making this woman happy.

"Oh God," she whispered when she came.

He couldn't help but grin, knowing he'd pleased her. He might have found a new type of crystal today, and that had been glorious, but pleasing Goldie had been better.

She lay there panting and he snuggled next to her, pulling the blankets around them.

"God that was good, Jack Boyle."

"Yeah it was."

She laughed but shook her head. "It's about to get better for you," she promised. "Take off your shirt," she ordered, putting it on when he handed it to her. "Sadly, it's too cold to be naked for long."

Then she helped him with his pants and proceeded to do exactly what he'd done to her, slowly teasing along his chest.

Licking his nipples, which felt amazing, before following the line of his hair down, down, down until she veered to the left and bit the edge of his hip, making him writhe and murmur what could have been "please," but he hoped he hadn't start begging so soon when she'd barely started touching him.

How long had it been since he'd wanted a woman this much? Maybe never. Goldie was his own precious metal.

She licked him everywhere but his cock, taking her time.

"Please," he begged again, finally breaking down, mindless under her ministrations.

She obliged him by finally slipping her beautiful lips over his head, just teasing him at the top.

"More," he gasped, needing so badly to find completion. Although he didn't want it to end so soon. He wanted it to last forever.

She stayed at the top first, simply mouthing his head over and over. But then she took him deeper, and it didn't take long for the pent-up need to explode over him in the best climax of his life, and God, he wanted to do it all over again. As soon as he recovered from the mind-blowing experience.

Afterwards, he pulled her up to his chest and snuggled her close, feeling closer to her than he'd felt to anyone in a long, long time.

It had been a long time, more than a year now he realized, maybe longer. He'd come to Mars and obviously that meant he'd be celibate, but before he'd left, he'd been so distracted. And while he would have preferred to be deep inside her, he found that this moment of relief had taken the edge off him to the point he could think about how amazingly lucky he was to even have found such a perfect woman for him on Mars. To have had this moment and for it to have been like this blew him away.

After finally stuffing his desire back into a box, contentment slipped over him and her as well he surmised, based on the pliant feel of her body as she draped herself across him.

He figured he wouldn't be able to rest with Goldie so near, that it would be too weird, but the minute he closed his eyes, he was out, sleeping the sleep of the dead. It was one of the best slumbers of his life.

<hr>

Margo woke up with the new morning sun hitting her eyelids, taking a long moment to study Jack Boyle, who was still asleep beside her. He was even more good looking without the slightly grumpy frown he tended to wear, made worse, she was sure, by the visiting TV contestants.

She still could barely believe she'd slept with the geologist of her dreams. Well, not slept-slept, but fooled around.

Orgasmed.

Jack. Boyle. Flopping on her back, she stared at the station ceiling, unable to stop grinning while she listened to him breathe. For the first time in her life, she understood why people suddenly broke into song or danced with joy.

It was so good, it was all she could do not to wake him up and do it again.

Part of her was embarrassed that she's been such a hussy, climbing on him and outlining exactly what she wanted. But she was proud of herself, because by speaking up, she'd had a mind-blowing experience she could take back out and relive for the rest of her life.

Since it felt cruel to wake him when he was sleeping so soundly, she slid out of bed, threw on her clothes, and went in search of coffee. As the water heated on a camp stove they'd brought, she rooted around and found two mugs. When she closed the cabinet door, she could see the outline of her tousled hair, the swollen lips, and her love swept appearance in the glass.

She touched her lip with a slightly shaking hand, unable to resist grinning at herself. They were in danger of dying and all she could think was I slept with Jack Boyle!

When she went back to the futon, Jack was awake, blinking at her, maybe a little confused as to how he'd gotten here.

"Coffee?" she asked, offering a mug.

"You're amazing," he said.

She felt amazing. An odd sense of peace filled her. As if things were finally right. Which was stupid, because nothing was right.

"No error message. I think it made it through," she said, sitting down when he patted beside him, cradling her own mug with both hands.

He leaned into her space to give her a long, deep kiss a feeling of need stirring deep inside her, but lazily, as if it wasn't all that pressing. "We should get back," he said when he came up for air, "But I really don't want to go."

"Me neither," she said, going in for another kiss, and lacing her free hand into his hair to pull him even closer to her.

She wanted to hang out and see Mars with him, hear all his stories, see everything he'd discovered so far. She wanted to have sex with him. Lots of sex. On Mars. With Jack. F'ing. Boyle. A smile spread across her face at the thought and she pulled away from the kiss to look at him. They were both breathing heavily, caught up in a haze of their attraction and mutual need. The sensible scientist side of her kicked in soon enough though, as thoughts of the tasks that lay before them started to creep into her mind. "Hopefully we won't run into any trouble, but I suppose we should leave early, just in case."

They both silently sipped their coffees, neither racing to go anywhere.

"Okay," he said on a sigh, putting down the mug. "We should go."

The hiss of an airlocked door opening made them both jump to their feet, Margaret spilling coffee in her haste. Jack took a step forward when another hiss signaled the entry door opening and a man walked through.

Beside her, Jack froze. "What the hell are you doing here?"

CHAPTER ELEVEN

"Sit," the man said, and his tone had so much command that Margaret obeyed.

Jack did not. "What are you doing, Haxley?" he asked, his whole body coiling into a tight spring.

Haxley must have seen the coming danger too, because he pulled something from his pocket, the action so swift she didn't register what he held at first, because she was too busy trying to match up the man she'd seen in science articles and on the console screen yesterday to the person before them.

She knew who Walter Haxley was—everyone who knew anything about Mars did. As a weather expert, he studied the seasons and wind patterns on the planet, although she hadn't seen anything from him lately. He'd been the first to find private funding to develop his own station and the first to take on sponsors. The commercials he'd been in before he'd left Earth still ran once in a while, and she occasionally still saw him giving weather reports from his station, which she'd always thought was a bit cutesy, but she'd still tuned in for them anyway.

"I said to sit, Boyle." This was a very different Walter Haxley from yesterday. Gone was the scared trembling and the dirty face. In fact, the hand that held an odd-looking gun was rock steady as he aimed it at them.

She tried to make sense of the gun, her brain having trouble with the stickup-like feel of the situation.

Thank God they'd been so cold, they'd gotten fully dressed this morning. Because this would be much worse if she still wore only Jack's shirt. She'd almost been tempted to see if she could interest Jack in a quickie. She'd warmed up to the idea even further after the amazing kiss he'd planted on her.

Jack held up his hands as he sat next to her on the sofa, the storm cloud of anger on his face belying the placating gesture. "You can't just kill us and get away with it."

"Of course I can. You're the one who said he'd been attacked by Russians in all your communications." He waved his gun. "You surprised me, Jack. You made it all the way here despite the fact I blew up your rover. And somehow you managed to have another rocket coming, when you were supposed to be starving to death. Very inconvenient."

"I weep for you," Jack said, his gaze searching Haxley's face.

She could almost see his intelligent mind looking for a way out of this mess. And she had to admit, if she had to pick anyone to be in this situation with, Jack Boyle was her number one choice.

What she didn't understand was why Walter Haxley was threatening them. It seemed crazy to think he'd set this elaborate plan in motion, because there wasn't an upside she could see. Blowing up Jack's rover and their rocket—it made no sense.

"So, there were no Russians. This has been all you from the start?" Jack asked.

"It was me." Haxley didn't look like he was gloating. In fact, his tone had a whine of apology in it. "I have problems but no resources to solve them. I need your stuff, Jack. It all comes down to that."

Jack frowned, showing he'd heard Haxley's whine, too. "You did it all. My rover, the rocket, the crazy com where you said you'd been attacked."

"All of it."

"Why?" Jack asked, which was Margaret's question too.

"Because you were supposed to be out of money months ago," Haxley raged, his emotions changing so quickly, Margaret flinched. "But somehow, even with all your grants drying up, you've managed to keep yourself afloat. And when I saw you had a new rover, I had to go check out Station 7 to see what else you'd been hiding from me."

"You went to my station?"

Margaret knew that couldn't be true. They'd talked to everyone last night, after they sent the messages. Russ would have told her if there had been a visitor and his demeanor had been as relaxed as ever. There had been no sign he'd been forced to lie. He'd been the same bordering-on-stoned guy he'd always been. And if they couldn't travel at night, neither could Haxley.

"And what did I find?" Haxley went on, his tone edging into hysterical. "A bunch of women filming a reality TV show!" His fingers grew white on the trigger. "I forced some idiot named Lynette to tell me how much she paid you, but that shouldn't have kept you going. It wasn't a small amount, but you should have folded already. I want to know where else your money is coming from before I kill you."

If he knew about Lynette, then he must have shown up after the call. Margaret suddenly got a bad, bad feeling, fear washing over her. He'd killed three of the contestants already. "You didn't kill them, did you?"

Jack's hand gripped her knee in warning, but she had to know.

"They'll die if I don't get the answers I need from your boyfriend here."

Which meant they were still alive. She blew out a breath and tried to let Jack handle this, since he knew Haxley best.

Jack shrugged his shoulders as if loosening up for a fight. "You want me to tell you, but if you're going to kill me, why would I share my secrets?"

"Because I'll kill your woman if you don't," Haxley said pointing the gun at Margaret.

She hissed in a breath and tried to master her fear. She wasn't going to die here on Mars if she could help it. The important thing was to stay grounded and not panic.

Jack shrugged. "You'll kill her anyway. You have to. Besides, she's not my woman. She's just some bimbo I picked up during filming."

"I'm not a bimbo," she hissed, because she figured Margo would say that, although she was only half acting. Being judged for her looks had always been a pet peeve. She appreciated Jack's attempt to take her out of the crossfire, but she wanted to know what the hell was going on here. Was Haxley working with the Russians?

"Hey," Haxley said, waving a hand at her. "Boyle's always been an idiot. Forget him. You can live with me."

Disgust nipped at her, the thought of spending the night in his bed making her sick to her stomach. She kept looking at Jack, not wanting Haxley to see her true feelings. It was time to be Margo again. Margo would handle this like any girl would, and since Margaret really had never been a normal female, she would need Margo's help.

Jack gripped her knee but the arrogant look was still on his face.

"You have to know that there was nothing between us," Jack said, his voice empty, as he turned to her. "You were supposed to leave tomorrow." He dismissed her by focusing on Haxley once more. "You should let all the TV people go on the shuttle. You don't want their blood on your hands."

Margo's heart tumbled at Jack's chivalry. He was willing to sacrifice his own life for her to get on the shuttle.

"Maybe I will let them go, along with your girlfriend, if you tell me how you've been funding your station."

"Guarantee me they'll go on the shuttle and I'll tell you."

Margo sucked in a breath. There was no way Jack should trust Haxley. The wide-eyed stare and sweat beading on his face screamed that something was very wrong. Mentally.

"I give you my word," Haxley lied, so obviously even she could see it.

"Why are you doing this?" Margo asked, unable to keep quiet. "You're famous and well respected."

"Because I need money for some very important repairs and I can't get a single grant with him taking everything. I got here months before him, but he's all the magazines and papers can talk about. You would think he's the second coming of Einstein." Haxley waved his gun. "Hell, even one of you TV stars jumped in the sack with him."

"I didn't—" she started, but of course she had. And she'd been about to do it again.

"Don't lie to me. Your hair is a rat's nest on the back of your head. I might be old, but even I know what just-fucked hair looks like."

Margo touched the back of her head, finding it snarled into a mess. She smoothed it before she could stop herself, dropping her hand when Haxley snickered.

She tried to get back on track. "But that doesn't give you the right to hurt Jack."

"Look at you. The man just insulted you and you're still on your knees for him. Boyle inspires that in everyone. It's pathetic."

Margo flinched at that sexist insult. What the hell? That wasn't all right. She wasn't used to such blatant sexism in a fellow scientist. Innuendo yes. Childish puns, undoubtedly. But blatant had been out for years.

———

Jack wanted to drive his fist through Haxley's teeth for insulting the women he'd fallen in like with. Because while he felt all warm and smushy about Margaret Carson, he wasn't silly enough to think it was anything but a deep, abiding interest. But he was also self-aware enough to realize they had something going here. The possibilities he could have with this woman were endless and he wasn't going to let anyone kill her.

The pieces had finally started to click together. Haxley had obviously gone off his rocker and he wasn't going to let Jack go and therefore he couldn't let Margaret go either, so freeing them wasn't going to happen.

Haxley held a zoot gun. The gun had been developed to fire in the lighter atmosphere of Mars to protect them from unknown predators or who knows what. Jack had never carried his because all that seemed to live here besides the odd virus or bacterium, was rocks. It should, however, be less accurate inside the station, since the atmosphere here was closer to Earth's density. Still, Jack didn't want to take the chance Haxley might kill them by luck or because the gun was accurate enough to get the job done.

"Where are the other two people from your station?" Jack asked, wondering if Haxley was on some sort of a rampage and had killed his staff.

"Richard really did die," Haxley said, looking momentarily sad about it. "He was electrocuted in the mechanical hut. An accident, I assure you."

"And Ellen?" Jack hoped the likable atmospheric scientist hadn't joined Richard in the hereafter.

Haxley shrugged. "She and I had a momentary difference in opinion, so I locked her in the supply closet. She'll come around. She just needs some time."

Jack thought fast. He had to come up with some way to get near the old man so he could overpower Haxley. Because the lightning-fast mood changes and the paranoid plotting were signs this wasn't going to end well. Maybe Haxley had Red Meningitis.

On the bright side, he hadn't killed them yet and Jack wasn't going to let him.

"You'll let Margo go if I tell you how I'm getting my money?" he asked again, setting the scene for his next move.

Margaret sat forward beside him, but he gave a tiny shake of his head, hoping she saw his plan when she realized where he was going.

"I promise," Haxley said.

Jack suppressed a sigh, disappointed his nemesis hadn't at least tried to lie convincingly. "It's in my pack," he said. "May I?" He pointed to his stuff still sitting in a pile beside the door, not wanting to startle Haxley and end up getting shot.

"Stay there!" Walter waved his gun around wildly.

Jack held out his hands in a placating gesture and settled firmly into the couch. "I'm not going anywhere."

The older man backed over to the packs and stood beside them as if he wasn't quite sure what to do. Then he dumped both bags out, items scattering everywhere with the force of his motion.

Chocolate bars covered the top of the pile from Margaret's pack and Jack glanced at her, lifting a brow. There were a lot of them, maybe twenty in all. Someone had a chocolate addiction.

She shrugged sheepishly.

"Follow my lead," he mouthed to her.

She nodded.

When Haxley had everything out of every pocket, he straightened. "There's nothing here," he snarled. "You've tried to trick me."

"There is, actually," Jack said. "Right by your left shoe."

Haxley searched around and brought up a rock. "This?"

"Yes."

"It's quartz," Haxley huffed.

"It's not. It's a diamond. I've been selling them."

Haxley held the crystal up to the light. It caught the rising sun from the viewport and spread a pretty rainbow across the floor. He stared at it in awe. "There are diamonds here?"

"I've been selling them slowly. I don't want to flood the market."

"Damn," he said, still staring at the rainbow, his eyes ringed with black circles from lack of sleep, his clothes hanging from his body.

Jack realized whatever was wrong with the old man had been going on for a long time. "Have you been feeling okay?" he asked.

Haxley's gaze snapped up, his eyes narrowing. "Don't start with that Red Meningitis crap." He waved his gun, getting agitated again. "You and Ellen need to stop harping on that. I told her and I'll tell you. I don't have it."

"Okay, okay," Jack said, holding out his hands in a placating manner again, wishing he wasn't trapped on the sofa. "But if you did, it's easily cured by taking antibiotics."

"What are the symptoms?" Margaret asked.

"Left untreated, it causes hallucinations, brain damage and kidney failure. Weight loss," Jack added, nodding at Haxley. "And lack of sleep."

"I'm sleeping fine," Haxley said, staring at the rock in his hand. "Tell me how to get to your stash," he ordered, bringing up the gun. "Right now."

Jack needed to get close to have his shot. "I'd have to show you. It's hidden."

Haxley pursed his lips, then turned to Margaret. "You." He waved the gun. "Into that chair."

Margaret flinched back into the couch.

"Wait," Jack said, standing to cover her.

"Stay back," Haxley shouted, his control obviously fraying. "The bimbo sits in this chair." He pointed at the one by the console. "Then we take your rover to this stash of diamonds."

"He can't drive my rover," Margaret said, standing, gripping Jack's arm to move him out of the way. "No one drives my rover but me."

"What?" Haxley asked in confusion.

"I think you should let me drive it this time," Jack said, annoyed that Margaret wasn't following his lead after she just told him she would. But what did he expect from her? She wasn't someone who would cower behind a man.

"Not a chance," she said. "That's a two million dollar prototype. I'm not going to let you wreck it."

He leaned close to whisper, "We're in a situation here, Goldie. This is not the time to get territorial."

"Forget it. You're not going anywhere in my rover," she said, through gritted teeth.

"That's ridiculous." At least Jack didn't have to worry she'd fall to pieces, since she was obviously too stubborn for that.

She shook her head. "Not happening. Only I drive."

Jack would be amused if this wasn't such a serious situation. "You are one stubborn woman, you know that?" Strangely, he found he liked her that way.

"Yeah," she said. "I do."

"Both of you shut up," Haxley ordered. "She sits on that chair." He pointed again. "Forget the rover. We'll take my ship." He pointed his gun and held it steady on Margaret, his patience obviously fraying.

She walked across the room as if she had to force herself to take every step. It was better if she stayed here. If he and Haxley ended up dead, she could drive back to Station 7 alone.

Haxley tied her to the console chair, which showed his mind wasn't working very well. That chair rolled and meant that Margaret could go anywhere in the room. He tied her tight, then gestured with his gun for Jack to proceed with him through the door.

Jack took one last look at the woman he hoped with every cell of his being he'd see again. Then he walked away, ready to do battle.

It was only as he was climbing into his space suit that Jack wondered what ship Haxley was referring to.

CHAPTER TWELVE

*M*argaret couldn't believe they'd left her tied to a chair. What the hell? And the old guy had done a really good job, too. He'd pulled her wrists behind her back, then zip tied them around the post that attached the backrest. The position put her arms at such an odd angle, her shoulders ached already and her hands were beginning to go numb.

One thing she knew, she wasn't waiting for someone to come save her.

Not that anyone would. No one at Station 7 had a working rover, let alone the skills to drive it. Only Jack and he wasn't going to be back any time soon. If at all. She clamped down on the thought and tossed it away. This wasn't the time to dwell on the worst-case scenario.

She rolled across the living room, inching forward with her feet. Then she realized she could go faster backwards, pushing off and gliding. It took her all of a minute to make it to the kitchen.

Ha! I'll be out of this so fast, I will catch up to Haxley before he's too far from the station. I'm really getting the hang of this spy thing.

Then the reality of her situation hit her and she groaned. She stared at the knife block wondering how she would get the knife into her hand, which was behind her back.

Time pressed down on her. She had to do this quickly, so she could catch up with Jack and Haxley. She knew where they were going. It would take half a day's drive, true, but Jack needed her. Haxley might kill him. The thought brought a feeling of both worry and panic. She couldn't let Jack be harmed, and it wasn't just that they'd had some sort of sex last night. Okay, so they weren't dating. He'd fooled around with her only because he thought she was going to leave tomorrow on the shuttle. Or that the Russians were going to annihilate them.

But while there weren't any Russians, that didn't mean Haxley wouldn't kill them all. Something was obviously very wrong with the man. He'd been jumping from emotion to emotion like a hot potato. And the color of his face, the dark circles, and the weight loss all said his health was in decline.

Which brought her back to the situation at hand. Before she could rescue Jack, she'd have to get off the chair she'd been tied to.

She knew Jack had been lying to him when he said they were diamonds, because he'd told her in the cave it was probably a type of quartz. But Haxley believed he'd seen diamonds, and she'd thought the rainbow from the sunlight had been a nice touch.

Step one of the plan—get free. Step two—race to the cave to save Jack. Unless Haxley's ship was significantly faster than her rover and they were gone before she could get there. Which was a large possibility if he had some kind of spacecraft. Like the one she'd seen yesterday.

Although, it hadn't gone fast when it had flown near them. It had moved about the speed of her rover. Which should have been too slow for flying, but it moved along just fine. Perhaps it had some sort of anti-gravity system. For a moment, Margaret dropped into the possibilities of that before ripping herself back to her current reality.

Studying the knife block, she tried to imagine how she could draw out the knife and concluded the only way was with her teeth. Planting her feet, she practiced standing with the chair attached to her ass. The chair made her seriously unbalanced. She wobbled and clunked backwards, the chair gliding away from the counter. She inched back into place and tried again.

Keeping upright by using her stomach muscles for balance, she leaned over the counter and her teeth almost closed around the knife. The chair tipped her and she fell back again, gliding even further away.

There was nothing to do but silence her screaming internal voice that begged her to hurry and repeat the process.

She tried again, this time managing to smash her nose into the knife block to take hold of a handle. She pulled the knife out.

Exhausted, she flopped into her chair, trying to pant while still maintaining her grip with her teeth.

Attempting to breathe through her nose, she wondered how the hell she was going to transfer the knife into her hands, which were tied behind her back.

For a moment, she despaired.

<hr />

Outside, Jack stared at the ship in the courtyard, incredulous. "Haxley, where the hell did you get this thing?"

The ship was the same one he'd seen the day his rover had been destroyed. It was matte black, conical in shape, the lines so smooth, it looked like a giant egg sitting before them. There wasn't an obvious door, or any break at all on the outside. And it weirdly reflected the land around them, almost, but not quite, blending into the background. It was so alien, so unlike any other craft Jack had ever seen, it made him instinctively recoil.

"I found it." Haxley caressed the smooth side. "She's a beaut isn't she?"

A bad feeling rolled over Jack. "You found it where?"

"None of your business," Haxley said, suspicion lacing his voice as he spun to face Jack, flinging out his arms protectively.

Jack had never seen any craft even remotely like this. And by the stubborn set of the old man's mouth, he wasn't going to tell Jack where it came from. So instead, Jack tried to get information another way. "If you're so hard up for money, why didn't you sell it?"

Haxley gaped at him, horrified. "I would never sell it. It's my friend."

"Your friend," Jack repeated cautiously, wondering just how badly Haxley had lost it. Hallucinations were a bad sign, although Jack had to admit the craft was a physical reality. "How do you open it? The outside is perfectly smooth."

On a dime, Haxley's mood shifted again to one of a proud parent. "It took me months to learn," Haxley said, his voice brimming with excitement. "I touched it and hammered at it and nothing. I didn't even scratch the outside. Then finally I did this." Haxley put his hand right in the middle of the side of the egg and pushed inward.

A round door cracked into existence, pushing back into the craft, then sliding into the wall as if by magic.

"Wow," Jack said unenthusiastically, liking this even less.

Since childhood, Jack had known there had to be other intelligent life forms out in the universes. It made sense that humans weren't the only ones. But he'd long ago thrown out any worries of aliens invading Earth. The likelihood was just too small, in his opinion. But now he stared at something so alien and amazing, it was conclusive proof there were others out there. And those others had made it next door to Earth.

Plain and simple, Jack feared it.

"And look at the equipment," Haxley was saying, gliding an arm across the opening to encompass the inside of the ship as if he were a saleswoman at a car show.

Fighting the urge to run, Jack leaned inside. The scientist in him that had to see warred with more basic instincts. "How did you figure out how to fly it?"

Haxley climbed in and beckoned Jack to follow him. "It took me forever, but then I discovered this." He picked up a strange helmet that wasn't exactly the shape of a human skull, flaring out wide to the sides before coming back in, as if to cradle a sideways hammer instead of a normal head. Wires came from all sides, attaching it to the ship, like some sort of weird hair. "And when I put it on my head," he did so, sliding it over like a toque, his neck wobbling a bit under the weight, "everything lit up."

Around them, the whole ship came to attention, small pinpoints of light running up and down the walls in columns. Jack resisted the urge to climb back off the ship. Because whatever this was, it was dangerous and Haxley had obviously crossed the line into madness if he was doing all this for the sake of the ship. The thing Jack didn't know was if the ship had caused his mental lapses or if Haxley had gone mad on his own.

In order to save everyone, including Ellen, who Jack hoped was still alive locked in a closet at Station 5 and not dead from starvation, he had to take Haxley's gun from him and get this ship safely secured where a team from Earth could study it. Which wouldn't happen if Haxley killed him, then blew up the inbound resupply shuttle. He had to protect the others.

Haxley fiddled with a strap. "Although it took me quite some time to adjust it to fit my head size. It was far too large at first."

The cockpit had two seats growing out of the floor without any seams, as if the ship had been cast from one, huge mold. Surrounded by panels of lights and instruments, Haxley turned his head and everything flickered. The door slid into place, bumping into Jack, pushing him further into the craft.

Well, he wasn't getting off now.

He peered closer at the panels. No knobs or buttons or anything a human could interact with lined the walls. "How does it work?" he asked, almost dreading the answer.

"I just think at it and tell it what I want to do. Isn't that amazing?" Haxley patted the panel before him as if it were a beloved pet.

"It didn't cross your mind that connecting your brain to an alien ship was a bad idea? Because this is obviously not technology from Earth." Jack ran a hand over the seat. It had the texture of a super hard plastic, but yet was warm and a small amount of energy wafted from it.

As if the ship was alive.

"This ship might have started out as alien, but it's mine now. I told it only to respond to me, and it promised to follow only my orders," Haxley said, his eyes lighting with a fanatical gleam. "So, don't try to steal it, Boyle. It won't work for you."

"I would never dream of stealing it." Jack wondered if that were true, but didn't plan to test it. There was no way he would ever put that helmet on.

The craft scared him on so many levels. It looked brand new, but Haxley had said he banged on the outside. Yet there were no dents or even scratches. Perhaps it was made out of some sort of alloy that never decayed? In which case, this ship could have been left on Mars for centuries, it's crew long dead.

And Haxley really believed the ship would only follow his orders because he told it to. If that wasn't crazy Jack didn't know what was.

"Where do we go? And don't think you'll fool me, Boyle."

"The spot is about halfway between here and Station 7." The cave would be an ideal place to strip Haxley of his gun and overpower him. Jack pulled up his data link and handed over the coordinates.

"With these, I could go without you," Haxley said, excitement building to the point he appeared to vibrate with it.

"Then leave me here," Jack said, hopeful that Haxley was altered enough to do so. He could go back inside and set Margaret free.

"He's trying to trick me, so I won't find the diamonds," the old man mumbled. "We'll get there and it must be hidden, so we won't find it and he'll have all the diamonds for himself. But we must have money to get the supplies you need to fix yourself."

Fear crept up Jack's spine. Haxley was much worse off than he'd thought. Because it appeared he was speaking to the ship.

Haxley cocked his head as if he were listening, the wires from the helmet sprouting off in several directions, making him look utterly insane. "Take us to these coordinates and he'll show us where they are. We'll do what we have to so you are fixed. I promise."

Suddenly, the whole front of the ship turned translucent, showing the surrounding terrain. The ship rose, as if to do Haxley's bidding, rocking Jack so he staggered back and caught himself against one warm wall. And they were off, moving slowly across the terrain, only a few feet above the surface.

Jack lowered himself to sit on the gently glowing green floor, trying to wrap his head around what was happening.

After a while, Jack stopped being scared and asked, "Why isn't it going faster?" Because an alien craft this advanced should be capable of sonic speeds.

"It's hurt," Haxley said sadly, patting the panel beside him. "It needs my help to fix itself."

"You're talking as if it's a sentient being."

Haxley grinned madly at him. "Oh, it is. It's alive, just hurt. I'm going to save it."

Holy shit, Jack thought.

C_____

After a few minutes of lolling in hopelessness and a feeling of doom, Margaret shook off her despair and figured out a plan.

She needed to drop the knife, then flip her chair over on its side. From there, she could grab the knife with her hands behind her and saw herself free. A simple plan for a simple problem.

Only the stupid chair wouldn't topple over.

She'd rolled back over to the rug, figuring that would cushion her fall a bit, and dropped the knife on the floor. Then she tried to flop over on her side, but all she seemed to be able to do was make the chair bounce back and forth on its casters. That motion scooted her away from the knife. She figured moving to the knife with the chair attached to her would be hard, so she wanted to stay close.

Part of the problem was that she didn't want to get hurt in the fall, so she'd been timid in her attempts. But now she knew she had to put her all into it and really commit. Time was ticking away. This was no moment for hesitancy.

With all her might, she screamed, "Ahhh!" and flung the chair sideways.

The chair smacked over on its side like a ton of bricks and Margaret landed with a smash.

"Son of a bitch," she moaned, her shoulders feeling as if they'd ripped from their sockets. She panted through the pain, waiting for it to subside.

When she was able to take stock of her surroundings, she realized she'd fallen halfway along the couch, which put her much further from the knife than she'd wanted to be. "Can nothing go right?" she asked, annoyed beyond belief. Because really, this was ridiculous.

Then she kicked her feet backwards, digging into the rug for leverage, and slowly worked her way to the knife, dragging the chair with her.

Her right hand scrambled a bit before she had the hilt firmly in her hand. Maneuvering it was tricky, but she finally had the blade in place.

On her first saw, it slipped and cut her pointer finger.

"Dammit," she moaned, dangerously close to losing her cool. *Get it together, Margaret. No panicking.*

She tried again and this time it worked.

Landing felt like he rode a feather. Just a puff of dust and they were down as gently as could be. The door opened and the front windshield turn opaque again.

"We'll be back. No, no I promise. As soon as we can," Haxley said to the ship.

Jack climbed out, taking a quick look at his oxygen reserves. He didn't have enough to make it back to Station 7, or he'd just hit Haxley over the head with a rock and take off running.

Instead, he pointed to the cave. "This way."

As they got nearer, Haxley grew suspicious, peering inside without entering. "You playing a trick on me?"

Jack pulled his flashlight from his pocket.

Faster than he thought possible, Haxley had the zoot gun out and aimed at him.

"Whoa," Jack said, and flicked on the flashlight. "Just a light. See?" He pointed it into the cave, lighting up the back wall into an awesome display of crystal.

"There they are!" Haxley exclaimed triumphantly, wiggling through the entrance without another thought about Jack and his flashlight.

Now that Haxley had the diamonds, he didn't need Jack anymore, so Jack had to act fast to make sure the other man didn't just shoot him.

"Haxley," he said, following him into the cave, planning to grab the gun while the other man was distracted. "I have to confess I lied to you."

"What," Haxley said still staring at the wall in wonder. "So many of them."

"I lied. Those aren't diamonds." Although Jack thought they were worth much more than any Earth gem. "I think it's a new type of quartz."

"You…lied to me?"

"Yes." Which was only fair since, Haxley had blown up his rover and tried to kill him. Would kill him, if he could.

Haxley must have believed it, because his shoulders fell and the gun hung useless at his side. "That's really awful of you, Boyle."

Jack dove for the gun, slamming into Haxley, who crumpled to the ground without resistance. Unprepared for such an easy defeat, Jack stumbled past him, catching himself on the far wall.

A loud crack sounded and it took a moment for Jack to realize Haxley had shot him, since he felt only a tug at his shoulder and not any pain.

Jack spun in a half circle with the impact. He tried to catch his balance, sinking to the ground. Scrambling, he covered the hole in his suit, trying to stop the oxygen leak.

Haxley stepped over him. "You've always been a jackass, Jack," he said, and left the cave without a backwards glance.

A sensor in his helmet beeped an alarm, making it impossible for Jack to hear if he'd stopped the leak, and a burn started in his left arm, painful fire racing over him. "Oh shit." If he didn't stop the oxygen loss, he'd be dead in minutes. Then his fingers slid and he realized he was bleeding. Even when he'd been in the military, he'd never been shot before.

He pressed hard, trying to stop the blood pooling in his suit and the air leak.

It took everything he had to remain calm enough to silence the alarm and carefully crawl forward until he was out of the cave. But Haxley and the ship were long gone. Exhausted, Jack fell on his back, careful to keep steady pressure on the tear.

Staring up into the blinding sun, he realized he'd never been in this big of a cluster in his life. Because he couldn't hold the hole closed and move without letting more O2 escape. Sooner or later, he'd weaken from the blood loss enough that he'd end up passing out. Then the temporary seal he'd created with his hand would open and he'd lose all the oxygen in his tank.

Jack was well and truly fucked.

CHAPTER THIRTEEN

*M*argaret pushed her rover like she'd never pushed it before, winding around boulders and bouncing over old washes and smaller rocks. She noted with some satisfaction that the suspension worked as she'd anticipated. She even cut through a deep wash to climb out, holding her breath as the rover expertly handled the descent and climb.

She flexed her bandaged hand, the small slice oddly painful, like a giant paper cut.

When she rolled into the area that contained the cave, she gave her rover an A for performance. She had a few things she'd need to adjust, the front struts could be a little longer, for example. But otherwise, she felt good about it.

What she didn't feel good about was that Haxley's ship was no longer here. If it had ever come. Maybe he'd taken Jack to his station and had locked him in a closet? No, she'd seen the glint of greed in Haxley's eyes. He would come here. She must have missed them while she had been wrestling free of the chair.

She rested her head against the steering wheel, all the stress from hours of aggressive driving weighing her down, wondering about her next step. If Haxley thought he had diamonds, would he go to Station 7 or his home base? She'd bet his station and she had no idea how to get there.

Glancing up to the sun, she figured it was midday.

A light flashed in her peripheral vision, drawing her notice. Was there something by the cave?

Probably just the sun reflecting on that quartz Jack had discovered earlier.

She debated for a bit, then figured her legs needed a stretch anyway and got out to check, knowing she was wasting time and yet not able to leave without making sure.

An oddly shaped rock moved before her.

She broke into a run as she realized the rock was a man.

"Jack," she yelled, dropping to her knees beside him.

He stared at her through the bubble of his helmet, his lips as blue as when she'd first seen him. His right hand pressed into his left shoulder, where blood leaked out around his fingers. Fear climbed through her, and suddenly all the possibilities she'd secretly had about them being together, all the building feelings she had for him and the respect she had for his career and her desire to see if this thing they had together would work, all flashed before her and she realized she didn't want to lose him—that she wouldn't lose him.

"Lay still," she said. First she had to stop the leak.

She bounded back to the rover, grabbed her duct tape and a rag, then bounded back. Kneeling again, she ripped off three strips, careful not to stick them together. She hung each from the bottom of her helmet, sticking the edge to the face shield, since she didn't know what else to do with them.

Jack's deep blue eyes stared at her as if she were a lifeline.

"Okay," she said. "On three, you lift your hand and I'll clean the blood off so this tape will stick and close the hole in your suit."

He blinked at her and she took that as a yes.

"One." This was going to be tricky. Too much oxygen loss and he wouldn't be able to recover.

"Two." But since they didn't have a choice, she had to do this. "Three."

He lifted his hand and she swiped the rag, then slapped on the tape. She ripped off a fourth piece before she was confident she had it.

For a moment, they both rested, her breathing as heavy as if she'd run a marathon.

Then she picked up his right arm to see how much oxygen he had left.

It rested on empty. All he had left was what was still in his suit.

"We have to get you to the rover. We can plug in your suit there and build back up your O2."

He nodded, the action feeble.

Jack felt like total hell. His oxygen level had been low for a while now and he wasn't sure he could move.

"Jack," Goldie, his savior, said. "You have to get up."

He stared at her. "You're beautiful," he said, raising his hand to touch her face shield.

"Whoa," she said, capturing his fingers and pulling then away. "Stay with me, Jack."

He grasped her hand and she hissed.

"What's wrong?" he asked.

"I hurt my hand. It's nothing. Listen, Jack, we have to get you on your feet."

He wanted to see her hand, see how bad she was hurt.

She knocked on his helmet, startling him. "Jack! Look at me. You have to get to your feet."

"You're a harpy," he told her, but he shifted his weight and managed to get his knees under him.

She wedged her shoulder under his armpit and he used her to climb to his feet. For a moment, they both staggered, but then they caught their balance and lurched to the rover, which had magically appeared right beside them.

"Your rover," he said, as she let him fall into his seat.

She slapped the close button and next he knew, she was beside him in the driver's seat. He must have passed out for a few moments.

"We need to decide what we're doing next," she said, playing with knobs.

He lost time again, then woke when she pulled off his helmet.

Air, glorious and amazing air, filled his lungs. He took deep, greedy breaths of it, realizing she'd managed to pressurize the rover so his helmet could come off.

"I have to look at that wound," she said, undoing some of the straps and seals of his suit. It took a while, but finally peeled back the fabric. "Oh wow." She closed her eyes in obvious relief. "It's just a bad graze."

As he lay there, he'd feared he'd been bleeding out. But looking at the shallow gouge in his shoulder, he knew he'd been fine. The injury hadn't even bled very much.

"I'm going to put duct tape on it until we can get a real bandage."

It seemed as good a solution as any, with them so far away from a first aid kit.

He watched her apply the silver tape.

"Jack, I know you're hurt, but we need a plan."

He took another big gulp of air and tried to think, but his mind was still fuzzy. "Haxley's ship is alien," he said, figuring he could tell her everything he knew and she could make the call, since her brain worked better than his did right now.

"Damn, you're still hallucinating aren't you?"

He frowned. "I'm not hallucinating," he said, his voice a bit snappish. He really should work on that. No one wanted to date an asshole.

"Oh thank God. You're back." She sunk into her seat in obvious relief.

"Haxley has an alien ship."

She studied him for a moment, then must have decided he was serious. "Alien how?" she asked.

"It's not technology I've ever seen. He controls it by wearing a helmet that connects his brain to the ship. I think it's made him insane."

"You don't think it's Red Meningitis?"

"I did, until I saw him talking to the ship. He really thinks it's conversing with him." And maybe it had been. After all, the ship itself existed, so why did he doubt that it could communicate?

"Wow." She sat quietly for a moment, thinking through that new information. "What are we going to do?"

"We have to get Haxley away from that ship. If it's taken over his brain, he deserves to live. I don't want to kill him if I don't have to." Jack had never been someone who wanted to take a life, but the crazy old man who had left him to die was dangerous to everyone on the planet.

"Would you kill him?" Goldie gaze was steady, without censure.

"To save us I would." He didn't even have to think about it.

She nodded, slowly as if she were thinking that one through. But it didn't seem to scare her. "So, what do we do next?"

"He's going to Station 7, so we have to, too."

She put the rover in gear and started without a question, following the vague tracks they'd left the day before.

As they rolled along, Jack tried to think but he had a headache, probably from the lack of oxygen. "Do you have a med kit in here?" He could really use an aspirin or something stronger.

"No. But I will remedy that as soon as possible. That was a major oversight it turns out."

"I have to admit, the thought of aspirin sounds so good right now I could weep."

She tossed him a quick, assessing look. "You don't look weepy. You look ready to eat nails."

"Well, that was the second time Haxley tried to kill me." Jack touched his shoulder. "It's like there are two of him. A pathetic old man and a crazy psychopath."

"How long do you think it will take him to get to Station 7? You'd think alien technology would make the trip in seconds."

"It's hurt."

"What?"

"The ship. It can't go fast and I think it had to stick close to the surface as well, because it barely rose a few feet off the ground. I'm not sure how long I was waiting for you. It seemed like forever."

"If he's going the same speed as the rover, then you guys only had a thirty-minute head start on me."

"That means he's what? Max an hour ahead of us, give or take a few minutes."

She nodded, agreeing with his logic.

"When we get to Station 7, there is one rule you have to promise to follow."

"What's that?" She worked them carefully through a crack in the ground, then back up the other side and he paused to let her concentrate.

When they reached the other side, he said, "We don't sacrifice ourselves for anyone else. We stay alive first. Just like a first responder on a bad accident scene. We can't save anyone if we throw our lives away."

At her pause, he pushed, "Promise me."

"I promise."

He dropped his head back to rest after the long exchange. "So, what do we do when we get there?"

"You're asking me?"

"You're all I've got," he said, so glad on many levels that he had her here with him.

"That's not a ringing endorsement."

"I'm not a ringing endorsement kind of guy." But he knew she'd saved his life.

"No, you aren't. But you're handy in other ways," she said, her tone just bordering on flirting.

He huffed out a laugh. "You are too. Like saving my bacon back there."

"I did, didn't I?" She hummed. "Our number one goal should be taking away the gun from Haxley so he doesn't shoot us."

"Yeah," he agreed.

"If he's at 7, then he has a lot of hostages he can bargain with."

"I've been thinking about that too." All those contestants could make great bargaining chips. Really high maintenance bargaining chips. Haxley would have his hands full, which was perfect for distracting him.

"If Haxley is inside, then we should disable his ship first."

"I'm not sure we can get inside it. He told me it agreed not to let anyone else fly it."

"If there is a way in, I'll find it," she said, so confident, he believed her.

"Okay then, you disable the ship and I'll disable Haxley." In the cave, he'd underestimated Haxley. He wouldn't make that mistake again.

"That sounds like a plan," she said, and went silent to concentrate on driving.

He spent the rest of the journey reprogramming their helmet channels to a separate bandwidth that wasn't shared by Station 7. The last thing he wanted was to have Haxley hear them over the intercom in the main building.

After a long, slow drive, they arrived, easing their way around the rocks and stopping before they got to the biodome, not wanting Haxley to see them if he was outside.

She scanned the area. "Stay here and I'll check the yard."

He almost fought her but then he realized he needed to conserve his strength. He was still a bit lightheaded from his near brush earlier.

She came back. "Everything looks quiet. Nothing moving at all."

He input the code to open a small door to the biodome. He wasn't worried that Haxley had set up any sort of warning. He hadn't had enough time and Jack hadn't had anything already set up like that. "Drive through those two pillars and around to the mechanical hut. We'll put your rover out of sight."

She zipped through and around the building, then climbed out to open the doors so she could drive through.

When they were safely inside he checked the oxygen readings to make sure the biodome was still functioning correctly. "The biodome can still support us without the suits, although at the low end."

"We're going without them then?"

"In a moment," he said, then framed her face in his hands and gave her a long, deep kiss that left his whole body weak and needy.

"Wow," she said, blinking up at him from her large, beautiful green eyes.

He traced her lower lip with his tongue, almost becoming lost in it all.

Then he made himself drop his hands and said to them both, "Later. We'll finish that later."

"Wow," she said again and touched her lip.

"And Margaret."

She blinked at him.

"Thank you for saving my life."

A slow smile spread across her face. "My pleasure."

"And for getting the generator up and running at Station 3."

"Wow, I'm getting some serious praise here."

"I'll give you more when we have more time." A piece of him wanted to lean back in and kiss her, stay here, and let the rest of the planet do what it would.

But that wasn't his way, and he knew it.

Jack stood, happy to find he no longer felt dizzy, then shimmied out of his battered suit, growling a bit as it chafed his duct-taped shoulder, abandoning his suit in a heap on the floor.

He watched Margaret load a bag full of tools into a backpack and sling it on her back.

He nodded to her. "Okay, let's do this thing."

They peeked out the door closest to the lab, both pausing to see what was going on in the courtyard. The egg rested in the middle, and he heard Margaret's small gasp through his headset when she saw it closely for the first time.

"Let's go," he whispered, knowing they didn't need to be silent, but not ready to speak in a normal voice yet. He felt like he was back in Afghanistan, doing a raid on a local village of insurgents. God, that had sucked. Worst time of his life, one he'd rather leave in the past. But it had paid for college, and grown him up fast, and he wouldn't be here without it.

They hustled to the side of the main building and pressed against a wall without windows. She'd be exposed until she made it to the far side of the ship.

Part of him wanted to go with her, but he had to let her disable the ship alone. His presence wouldn't add anything. She was the expert.

Instead, he held his breath as she ran across the short, exposed expanse and then he tapped in the code to his lab.

CHAPTER FOURTEEN

*M*argaret pressed her hand into the center of the ship, hoping what Jack had described would work for her.

Nothing happened. Damn, maybe it really will only open for Haxley.

She leaned her head against her hand…and a panel slid out of the way, as if it had melted into the right side.

Wow.

She paused to peer inside, awed by the sight. The whole ship was made out of one continuous piece of hard resin, the lines of it like modern furniture from the early 1990's. Two chairs grew up out of the floor and pointed toward a blank wall, as if it were missing a windshield.

She climbed aboard, and the door shut behind her, making her jump. She had a panicked thought that maybe she was locked in here forever, but she placed that fear aside, taking the bag of tools from her backpack.

How amazing would it be to spend days combing through an alien ship, unraveling the secrets of another race's technology. She couldn't believe her luck, getting to be the third human to experience this.

The helmet was sitting beside the left-hand chair, looking much like Jack had described to her.

She picked it up, studying it. Lights on it blinked twice in hello, almost as if the ship were telling her to put the helmet on.

Curiosity welled up as she wondered what it would be like to try it on, but she ignored the building desire. She had to disable the ship and her gut told her that the quickest way to do that was to separate the helmet from the vehicle. That would keep Haxley from communicating with the ship, if that's what he was doing.

Although if the ship really was communicating with Haxley as Jack thought, severing the connection to whatever link it had into his mind might leave the old man injured as well.

Studying the layout, she realized there wouldn't be cables if the helmet could operate without them.

She pulled the helmet out as far as it would go from the wall, lengthening the cables, studying them for any weaknesses. The wires were made of the same, hard, smooth plastic as the ship. There was no way to unscrew or unplug them from either the helmet or the hull.

She tried pulling the helmet free from the wall. Bracing against the chairs, she leaned all her weight against it.

They held firm, no sense of give at all.

Which meant she had to chop them apart. She dug in her bag for an awl and a hammer. Placing the edge of the tool against the cord, she hit it as hard as she could. The awl slid off without making a dent.

She sat back, staring for a long moment at the cord. Then reached for her blowtorch. It lit with a blue flame and the floor under her feet gave a small shiver, as if the ship didn't like it. Which was dumb. The vehicle wasn't alive. She put the flame to the cord.

The ship rocked sideways, throwing her violently against the wall. The blowtorch fell, still lit, to the ground, sliding away from her.

A loud whine filled the small space when the lit torch touched the floor, filling the space with a loud screech.

"Okay! Okay!" she shouted. "Let me put it out." She scrambled to flip the switch, extinguishing the flame.

The noise stopped immediately.

The ship was alive. And she'd hurt it.

The thought was so amazing, so insane, that Margaret lay quietly on the floor, unable to do anything but puzzle out this crazy reality. Someone, somewhere far, far away, had built this ship and maybe flown it here.

Or…birthed it.

She shivered at the thought.

But that was too farfetched for her scientific mind, so she decided it had been built and maybe the pilot had died, or had abandoned it, if Haxley was right and it was only able to fly at a reduced speed close to the ground. This sentient being had been left alone, unable to return to its home, stuck here. And she'd hurt it.

Feeling remorse, Margaret patted the ship and whispered, "I'm sorry."

It didn't answer.

She had to figure out what its intentions were, had to figure out how to separate it from Haxley for good and free the older man before he couldn't be saved and descended completely into madness.

For a few moments, she fought the idea, but really she knew she had no choice.

Slowly, knowing she could be making an irreparable mistake, she put the helmet on.

———

Jack peered through the small window he'd first seen Margaret through.

Haxley was nowhere in sight.

He opened the door and slid through.

Pausing to listen, he heard footsteps coming from the living room, so he ducked around the corner to the side hall.

Haxley entered, his movements jerky and agitated. "It has to be here," he mumbled. He opened Jack's map cupboard and began tossing the rolls out, ruining Jack's carefully compiled collection.

When that cabinet was empty, he opened the next one down and started throwing things from that.

Jack backed slowly down the side hall, then, when he could no longer hear Haxley, went looking for the contestants. He hoped they weren't dead already.

For such a small space, he had to search for a while, because his first tour through the kitchen, his bedroom, and living room hadn't turned up anyone. He went back to the closed storage door and threw back both locks. Opening it, he found them all squashed into the small space.

The light came on when he opened the door, a feature he'd put in to make sure no unnecessary electricity would be wasted.

Lynette opened her mouth, but he put his finger to his lips and she snapped it shut again. He leaned close. "Barricade yourselves into the kitchen. I'm going to try to talk Haxley down."

Lynette stepped out and started shooing the contestants toward the kitchen. "Good luck with that. The guy's insane. Totally bonkers."

"Yeah," Jack agreed, then nodded for her to go too. "Make sure they stay as silent as you can. You don't want to draw his notice."

Russ stopped by his side. "Want me to be your backup?" Russ asked, jumping a bit on his toes like an overweight boxer getting psyched up for a fight.

"Not right now. I may need you later."

Russ gave a worried nod and followed the others.

Then Jack went to his bedroom and rummaged until he located some zip ties, stuffing them into his pockets.

Going for simplicity, he figured he'd dive onto Haxley, knock the zoot gun out of his hands and tie him up. The old man was fast. He had to watch for that and not get shot again. Next time, he might not be so lucky. He picked up a chunk of basalt from his collection for luck and stuck it in his pocket.

Then he returned down the side hall and inched around the bend.

The sound of items crashing to the floor had him gritting his teeth. The old man was going to destroy his lab. He couldn't see him, though, so he inched closer.

Then closer still.

He peered carefully around the corner.

And looked right into the end of Haxley's zoot gun.

Shit.

"I want your money, Jack. I'm not kidding around," Haxley said.

The mad light in his eyes told Jack he was in serious trouble. "Haxley, I swear. I have nothing. Really. You can check my bank balance."

The old man gestured Jack into the room with his gun. "Show me."

Jack walked to the console, his shoulder blades tingling. At any moment, Haxley might shoot him in the back. He tapped the screen and brought up his accounting software.

Pointing to the balance, he said, "See? All I have left is what the show paid me."

Haxley growled, the sound feral. "That should have come to me! I have twice as much room at my station as you do. Picking Station 7 was short sighted."

Jack knew from what Margaret's brother had told him that they didn't want Haxley because they thought Jack had more television appeal, whatever the hell that was. But no way was he telling Haxley that. "I can give you their information and you can contact the producer. He's a guy name Hank Carson. Or," he said, warming to the idea of offloading Haxley onto Hank, "We can pitch a trip to Station 5 as one of the dates and tell them your fee. They want to have a bunch of locations where the contestants can be filmed out of their suits."

"Shut up," Haxley said.

Jack stopped talking, watching closely for an opening.

"Transfer all your money into my account," he ordered. "I want it all."

"Okay," he agreed, wondering if he could just pretend to transfer it, but the old man was so paranoid, Jack didn't think he could fake it. "What's your account number?"

"I," the old man stumbled. "I don't know." He seemed lost for a bit, then straightened. "We'll have to go back to my station and—"

The door to the courtyard opened and Margaret walked in.

Haxley swung his gun around, but Jack chopped down on his hand, sending it flying across the room. It bounced against the console. Haxley jumped to retrieve it, but Jack tackled the older man, sending them both skidding into a set of cabinets, hitting with a tremendous bang. Rolling on top, Jack held the older man down with his knees in Haxley's back.

"That hurts," Haxley moaned.

Jack wasn't falling for the old man's tricks. He'd already been shot once for his trouble. "I'll lighten the pressure if you stop fighting."

Haxley stilled, his breath heaving, and Jack used the opportunity to dig into his pockets for the zip ties. Then Jack wrestled the man's hands together behind his back and secured a zip tie around one wrist.

Without warning, Haxley fought like a demon, scrambling to get to his feet but Jack put all his weight on the back of Haxley's knees. The man screamed in pain and stopped struggling instantly.

Margaret dove in to help Jack put on the other zip tie, looping it through the one already secured on the other hand, then threading it into the catch and pulling tight.

Margaret crouched down to meet the old man's gaze. "Your ship is gone," she informed him.

Haxley stopped moving. "What?"

"Your ship left."

"No, no, it wouldn't leave."

"It did. I fixed it and it left," she said.

"No. That can't be true. It wouldn't leave me. You're lying," Haxley screamed, then started to cry.

She patted his shoulder. "It said to tell you goodbye."

The old man cried harder, as if his heart was breaking, the sobs so pathetic, it hurt Jack's heart to hear them.

Jack crossed to the console and started fiddling with dials.

"What are you doing?"

"Calling Station 5. Ellen might be stuck in the closet and if she is, we'll need to get a rescue mission together to let her out."

But it turned out Ellen had gotten out of the closet without their help. She answered Jack's call on the first ring, sounding relieved when Jack told her they had Haxley in lockdown.

A loud bell started to toll.

"Ellen, I'll call you later. We have visitors," Jack said, pressing buttons to cut the call.

"What is that noise?" Margaret asked.

"Your brother's shuttle is landing. The biodome is warning of an incoming ship and it's peeling back to allow entry. With the coms down, they had no ability to warn us they were going to land. Let's stash Haxley in the storage closet and go meet them."

CHAPTER FIFTEEN

$\mathcal{J}$ack's lab was filled to the brim with contestants, the Bachelor, the staff, the shuttle pilot, and Hank Carson, who stood grimly in the center of the room, listening to the whole tale unfold. He didn't ask questions, just listened, a live Ken doll looking both fashionable and in command.

"When I put the helmet on," Margaret was saying.

"That was a hell of a risk," Jack said, interrupting her, his heart hammering with fear that she'd put herself in jeopardy like that.

"I know. But the ship is alive and I couldn't communicate with it any other way."

"Do we have film of this alien craft?" Hank asked.

"We should," Jack said. "I have video feeds set up so I can keep watch outside."

Hank gave a brisk nod. "Go on, Margo."

She winced at the name. "When I put on the helmet, it told me what was wrong with it. Well, showed me I guess would be a better way to describe it. A part had broken off, as if it had been sheared right through. It's what had controlled the hyperdrive that allowed it to reach sonic speeds."

"Like it snapped off?" Jack asked, trying to reconcile that with what he'd seen in the ship. "Couldn't it just make itself a new part?"

"It told me it couldn't. And the scene it showed me was of a bad man slicing it off on purpose, trying to ground the crew it had carried here on Mars."

"Did the man look human?"

"Human-ish. It had a huge head though."

"I guess we aren't the only race with our share of Haxleys."

"Then what happened?" Lynette asked.

"I managed to attach it with duct tape. I told it that it might not stick, but when the two surfaces connected, a whole new panel lit up. And the ship rejoiced, because it could go home."

"Where is home, I wonder?" Jack's imagination took off and for a few seconds, he was lost in the possibilities.

"I didn't ask it, but now I wish I had," Goldie said. "I'm worried that a long journey will leave it stranded somewhere else, if the duct tape doesn't hold."

"What happened after you fixed it?" Hank asked, his tone impatient.

She shrugged. "I stepped off and it flew away. Just shot up into the air and was gone."

Jack found the video feed, rewound a bit, then let it play for Hank. The ship's departure was fast and furious, it's speed obviously restored. He'd been afraid of the ship, but now that it was safely away from him, he admired its sleek lines and amazing abilities. Jack wondered what the implications were now that alien life was confirmed.

"Rewind and play it slowly." Goldie leaned in and pointed. "See how there is no backwash from the engines? I was standing right beside it without any danger."

Jack rewound the footage and played it again.

"What is the power source?" she murmured.

"I don't know." Jack grinned, watching her expert mind take flight. "Wish it had stayed longer?"

"You know I do. I wish I'd thought to ask it questions, but all either of us wanted was for it to leave, I think."

"Where's Haxley?" Hank interrupted, losing interest in the ship.

"Storage closet," Jack answered, disappointed to see Goldie lose her train of thought. But he figured she'd spend the rest of her life thinking about what she'd seen. He knew he would.

"Where he put us," one of the contestants pouted.

"I almost wet myself, we were in there for so long," another said.

Hank nodded, his face sympathetic. "You were all terribly brave." He turned back to Jack. "I figure you owe me another ten days of filming."

"Wait, what?" Jack's brain skipped at this declaration. Hank Carson needed to take his contestants and go. Well, everyone but Margaret. She could stay. But his tolerance for filming was at rock bottom.

"Smith," Hank said to the pilot. "You have to leave when?"

"Three hours if we want to stay on schedule," the man replied. "Any more time here and you'll be charged for an extra day."

Hank hissed at that. "Okay, we have three hours to do three rose ceremonies, then we'll send all the losers home."

Jack tried to calm his rising panic. "You can't stay. I need you gone."

Hank was already turning away to organize his troops. "Not going to happen, Boyle. You signed an ironclad contract." He swung back to point at Margaret. "You did, too."

Lynette waved her clipboard. "Their clothes have been destroyed."

"Then we'll film in casual." Hank clapped his hands. "Let's move people. The clock is ticking."

Lynette stood mute for a moment, eyes narrowed at him as if Hank had plucked her last nerve. Jack secretly cheered. Then she turned on her heel. "I want all women in the kitchen for makeup on the double."

The ladies herded out.

Lynette jerked her head. "Including you, Margo."

"Not a chance," Goldie answered.

"She hasn't been voted off yet?" Hank asked, a little too incredulous for Jack's taste.

"No."

"And she's not going to be," the Bachelor said from where he still stood against the far wall.

Hank rounded on him. "Why the hell not?"

"You promised me I would get to choose."

"And you think you'd be happy with my sister? Are you insane? She'd make a horrible wife."

An angry wave rose over Jack. "Watch your mouth, Carson," he said, menacingly. Jack imagined how good it would feel to drive his fist into Hank's mouth. Must. Not. Hit. Goldie's brother.

Margaret's heart fluttered at Jack's old-school chivalry. "It's okay." She was still a bit high from fixing the alien ship. It was as if she'd spent her whole life waiting for that moment, like a surgeon who repaired a child's heart. Because the ship had seemed like a child to her. Its emotions were simple. It hurt and it was lonely. It wanted to go home, where it would be safe and loved. It had spent too long here, time going on and on while it waited for one of its kind to find it. But it never did. She'd wanted so badly to help it. And she had.

"No, it isn't. In fact, an apology is in order," Jack said, as if he really wanted to force Hank to give her one.

Hank turned to Lynette. "What the hell is going on here?" he asked, confused.

"You know what, Hank, it's your sister and your choice for the bachelor. You figure it out. I'm going to run the girls through makeup." She stomped away, clearly done with the whole thing.

"I'm still waiting for you to apologize to your sister, Carson. She stuck her neck out to save all your cast and crew and doesn't deserve your slander." The Jack Boyle standing in the room was hard as nails and had a deadly edge to him.

Hank studied Jack for a moment and must have concluded he was serious. He turned. "Margo, I'm truly sorry if I hurt your feelings."

She almost laughed at her brother's plight. He never apologized when he could charm his way out of trouble. "I accept your apology, Hank," she said, gravely. Because no matter what, she loved her brother and in the end, he'd sacrificed a lot to get her to Mars, risking his show in the process.

The unpleasantries done, Hank turned to Chad. "Tell me why you want to keep her. If you truly have interest in her, she'll stay in the game."

"Wait! What?" Then Margaret realized her brother no longer held testing her rover over her. "You can't force me to be on this show."

"Hush." Hank held up one finger in her direction, but didn't turn, giving Chad his full attention. "Chad?"

Chad's bravado fell in the face of Hank's willingness to negotiate. "I don't want her in, but I also don't want Misty out."

"It was my understanding you voted Misty out?" Hank said, making it a question.

"It was a mistake. We've grown close during this whole catastrophe."

"Good lord," Margaret said, unable to keep quiet. This was so contrived, she could scream. He'd already slept with Misty. Even thought he'd voted her out. If she had a man treat her that way, she would poke his eyes out. But then, she'd never wanted to be chosen from a group of women. She'd always wanted to meet someone and have the instant connection that made him know she was the one.

"Okay, so we'll have Margo have an accident and bring Misty back. Would that make you satisfied?"

"Yes, I believe it would," Chad said, sticking out his hand. "It's a deal."

They shook on it. "Do you still have your rose ceremony suit?"

"Yeah," the bachelor said.

"Get into it. We'll start the ceremony in a few moments. We'll tell the girls of Margo's demise, then have Misty reappear at the end of the ceremony. That will cause all kinds of drama."

Chad grinned. "Sounds like fun."

Hank nodded. "It will be."

After Chad left, Hank swung to her. "What's up with you and Boyle?" he asked, right in front of Jack.

She stuttered, trying to summarize something she wasn't really sure how to define. What was up with her and Jack? They'd fooled around and had struck up a friendship. Those were the facts. But it was more complicated than that and everything was so new, she wasn't sure where they stood. "We bonded while saving everyone's lives," she said tentatively, feeling weirdly exposed with Jack standing right there.

"We're dating," Boyle corrected, surprising her.

"We are?" she asked. She'd secretly worried this was a one night thing, but Jack didn't seem to have trouble saying it was more to her brother.

"Yeah," Jack said, his lips curving into a small, pleased smile. "We're seeing where this leads."

"Really?" Hank asked, his face saying that he couldn't believe it.

That sounded like an insult, so Margaret said, "Don't act so surprised."

"Margo, you haven't dated anyone in years."

"That doesn't mean I'm dried up and on the shelf," she said, annoyed. No one could irritate her like her family.

"Well, she's dating me now," Jack said, finality in his tone.

A girly flutter shivered inside her.

"Great!" Hank said, already losing interest. "We can talk about this fascinating topic later. I have filming to do now. Margo, pack your bags, because you're leaving in three hours with this shuttle."

"That's fast," she said, but she'd known this moment was coming, had in fact fought to get herself kicked off when Chad had wanted to keep her. Now she wished she hadn't said a word. She would have loved to explore what was blooming between her and Jack for a little while longer.

Margaret watched her brother walk away, the reality that she was really leaving sinking in. She had been so busy living in the moment, she hadn't thought about the future.

A future that wouldn't include Jack, because long distance dating never worked and when the distance was over fifty four million kilometers, it really wasn't feasible.

Stay, something inside her whispered. But while she might like Jack and he'd told her brother they were dating, which had been wonderful, she'd always promised herself she would never give up her career for a man and she wasn't going to start now. Because if she missed the University's budget meeting, her lab would end up with no funding, which would mean she'd have no lab. She'd have no place to modify her rover and everything she'd spent the last ten years working for would be over.

⟢⟶

From the other room, Jack could hear Hank coaching Chad about strategy for the next rose ceremony. They had to be standing right near the doorway. From the bits and pieces that filtered into the room, they were rolling out which order Chad should deliver the roses in.

He had three hours left with Margaret and he knew he had to make them count if he was going to change her mind. Once she left, it would be a long time before he saw her again. Even if he ended up shutting down his station, it would be months before he'd be Earth-side. So he wasn't going to spend what might be the last moments with her listening to Hank manipulate rose ceremonies.

"Want to go see the valley I've been collecting samples from? The view is the best thing I've seen on this planet." Well that was stretching it a bit. The best thing he'd seen on this planet was her. "We could be there and back long before the shuttle leaves."

The sad frown that had come with the news she only had three more hours dropped away as a smile bloomed across her face. "I could be talked into doing that."

"You want to drive?" he asked, trying his best to charm her, adding what he hoped was his most dashing grin.

She laughed. "You know I do."

So they shrugged into suits and she drove them out into the desolate wasteland that was Mars.

They talked about where he was in his research and how her rover was handling in the real environment it was built for the whole way there. Then they stood side by side, studying the red valley before them, her silence attesting to her awe. He loved that he could share this with her.

She sighed. "I should go."

He caught her arm when she turned to leave. "Stay," he said, knowing as he said it that it was right, because they were perfect together. "I may only have a couple months left. You could fully test your rover, maybe work on a new design." He studied her face, watching closely to see which way she'd lean. He realized he wanted her here more than he'd wanted anything in a long time.

He could see the wheels turning in her head. She was going to say yes. His whole body tightened in anticipation. He'd never wanted anything so badly before, not even Mars.

"Jack," she said, and his heart sank. "I have to get back to Earth. If I miss an upcoming budget meeting, I lose my lab. Then where would I work on my rover?"

"Here," he said, throwing out his arms. "Who needs a lab when you could have the real thing?"

She took a deep breath and shook her head. "I'm sorry, Jack. I have to go back. If I lose my lab, it will take me years to find another university that will give me what I currently have. It will set me back years in my career." She touched his arm. "Please understand."

Sadly, he did. But that didn't mean he liked it.

CHAPTER SIXTEEN

They were silent on the way back. She knew Jack wasn't pleased with her decision. Quite frankly, she wasn't happy either. But she had a lab at home, dammit, and if she didn't defend her funding, she'd end up losing it.

It amazed her how much she wanted to say yes to staying. She wanted to so badly. The fact was, Margaret had never done anything impulsive in her life. She didn't like impulsive decisions. Besides, only idiots threw caution to the wind, sacrificing everything for love.

Jack got out of the vehicle without saying another word and started for the mechanical hut door. Then he stopped and turned on one heel. "I know you have obligations back on Earth. But you've got an hour to change your mind and I hope you will." He took her arms, feeling far away since they were both in their space suits. "But either way, you're not done with me. I won't be up here forever."

Seeing him standing before her, a strong, intelligent man declaring his intensions made her heart hurt and she trembled. "Well, you know where to find me when you come home." But she knew distance wasn't kind to a shiny new relationship like theirs. They might be able to exchange the occasional message, but otherwise their relationship would be silent.

He nodded. "I do and I will." Without saying more, he left, leaving her standing there more torn than she'd ever been, part of her wanting him to try to talk her into staying.

Did she expect him to beg her to stay? Jack Boyle didn't beg. He commanded and promised. This was a man worth making sacrifices for, worth giving up things to be with.

She trudged into the station, her mind spinning on the possibility of simply staying on Mars. What if she let her ride home leave without her? She'd finish her rover here. If she lost her lab, she take the job that NASA kept offering her. It didn't have to be the end of everything, but perhaps a new beginning—one that might include Jack if things between them worked out.

But if she did this, she'd be risking everything she'd built for love.

She couldn't, wouldn't do it.

When she was out of her suit, she wandered into the living room to pack her things. Another rose ceremony was in full swing. Chad handed out roses, one by one, to the contestants, Misty standing proudly in the front row, already holding one.

Hank stepped forward. "This will be the last rose," he said in his deep announcer voice and stepped back.

Chad paused and slowly glanced at the two women remaining, back and forth until Hank tapped him on the arm to signal that he could speak again. "Amanda?"

Claire, the only one without a rose, began to cry, crumpling as she sobbed.

Instead of a squeal of delight, Amanda stayed where she was for a moment, then walked down to stand in front of the bachelor, wobbling a little on her extra high heels she'd had to wear since she was shorter than the rest of the cast.

"Amanda, will you accept this rose?"

Her jaw set. "Chad, I think you're an amazing man, but I'm really not feeling the connection I think we should have at this point in the show," she said, touching his hand but not taking the rose. "I cannot take your rose."

Chad blinked a few times, clearly struggling with her decision. He'd been coached for this, but it took a few moments for him to force out, "I understand. May I escort you out?" Chad presented his arm.

"I'd like that," Amanda said, as sweet as ever, her face crunched down in a worried frown that told Margaret she wasn't enjoying this.

Who would? Not Margaret, who had essentially told Jack she wasn't taking his rose either.

They left from the room arm and arm, Russ backing down the hall in front of them with a camera.

Hank whipped around to Lynette. "Did you know about this?"

Lynette jutted out a hip and rested a hand on it. "Were you not just complaining to me that this season was boring, despite the fact we are on Mars?"

"In the lab," Hank growled, stalking out

Margaret grabbed the few pieces of clothes she'd left behind when she'd gone to Station 3 and then walked to the lab to get the rest of her things.

"Chad is not supposed to be turned down," Hank was saying as she walked in. "The fantasy is he picks them."

"Well, there was a bump in the fantasy." Lynette's tone clearly said she didn't give two hoots that Hank was angry with this latest turn of events.

"It's your job to make sure there aren't bumps."

"Don't blame this one on me, Carson. It's not my fault Amanda doesn't like him because he slept with Misty. That's on your bachelor for being a man whore."

Hank held his head in his hands. "He was never supposed to be alone with any of them. That's a rule."

Lynette marched all the way into Hank's space. "You left me to deal with this insanity alone. I told you it was a bad idea for you to stay behind. That there were too many people for one woman to control and Russ is next to useless."

"Hey," Russ said from the camera bank.

"No offense," Lynette said, sparing him a quick glance.

"None taken," Russ answered, already focused on something else.

"Did I not tell you it was a bad idea, Hank?" Lynette asked.

Margaret slid around on the edges of the room trying to reach the pack she'd taken to Station 3.

"Yes, you did," Hank conceded. "But—"

Lynette talked over him. "Once I lost the rocket, I had no ability to keep them totally separate. That's not on me."

Margaret stuffed the clothing in her arms rapidly into her bag, hoping to escape before they saw her. Right now, they were totally focused on their fight, but that anger could fall on her if she didn't get out quick. Because her brother had met his match. Wow.

Hank rubbed his eyes. "How many more want to leave?"

"Most of them. I'm keeping them here by the skin of my teeth, reminding them they can't get on Paradise without my approval."

"Jesus Christ," Hank said and paced in a tight circle.

Margaret realized she had nowhere to go. She couldn't join the women in the living room and right now, those voted off had taken up residency in the kitchen. She belonged to neither group. Despondent, she slid down against the wall, figuring they were so caught up in their conversation she wouldn't be noticed.

"I did the best I could under the circumstances," Lynette said, losing a smidge of her righteous anger.

"I know you did."

"This whole thing has been fucked from the word go. I don't think even you can save it."

Hank stopped massaging his head, straightening. "You're wrong. Nothing is ever unsalvageable. Remember episode 32? We thought it was unredeemable, but we pulled it out."

Lynette tipped her head back and forth. "Maybe. But that was because everyone got food poisoning. Eventually, they all left the hospital and we could resume filming. This time is worse."

Well at least Margaret wasn't the only one who wasn't going to get what she wanted. It occurred to her that since she was going home, she didn't need to save her chocolate bars for an emergency. She rummaged around her bag until she found one.

"It's not time to give up yet." Hank said, his voice turning to steel. "What's the underlying problem?"

"There are several, but the number one problem we have is that they don't like him. And you know the audience can tell if they're faking, no matter how much we edit."

Margaret took a bite. Pure joy melted into her mouth. God, she loved chocolate. She was really blue about leaving. Why couldn't she put all her responsibilities aside and take a chance? For the first time in her life, she wished she was that person. She took another mouthful, feeling weepy.

Hank ran his fingers through his hair. "We're selling love here and to do that, we need them to be in love with him."

"We can't get that back. He's chosen Misty and they know it. Once you let her return, they decided the game was over."

Jack had chosen her, Margaret realized. To have someone who was the poster child for being a recluse ask her to stay with him was monumental. He wasn't making a spontaneous decision, either. She'd bet he'd thought it all out backwards and forwards and was one hundred percent sure he wanted her with him.

She looked down. The chocolate bar was gone. The foil lay forlorn in her lap. She still felt weepy. Well, she could diet later, alone on Earth, in her lab. She dug through her bag for another.

"How can we get this back? There has to be a way." Hank resumed his pacing.

"There isn't," Lynette said, and Margaret could tell she felt sorry for her brother.

"I need ideas, not naysaying, Lynette!" he said, desperation in every word.

Taking another bite, Margaret let the chocolate high spread through her, which was why she decided to add her thoughts to their conversation, despite her gut instinct to stay silent. "You could have a shortened show and have him pick Misty early over everyone else. Just end it now. Blow the viewing audience off their asses," she suggested, throwing out the most outrageous idea she could think of.

Hank whipped around. "What?"

"Just have another rose ceremony and have Chad throw away all the roses except one and give it to Misty." She chomped down on the chocolate bar, now completely out of control, tossing calories to the wind. "People would cry their eyes out. The only bachelor in history to be so in love, he threw away the game."

Margaret wished she loved someone that much. The thing was, she could fall that hard for Jack. They were perfect for each other, both scientists, both focused on learning, they would understand when the other needed to work late in the lab, could listen to long, drawn out, boring stories about grant funding woes. And, besides being sexy hot and one of the smartest guys she knew, Jack had Mars, the thing she'd always wanted.

Lynette and Hank were arguing back and forth, but Margaret wasn't listening, instead concentrating on finishing her current chocolate bar, like a woman on a mission. Eating it had gone from fun to feeling sick, but fuck it, she was getting drunk on sugar even if it killed her.

"It could work," Lynette said slowly.

"It could," Hank agreed. "And we could bring everyone home on this shuttle and save a shit ton of money by not needing another shuttle run."

"People would know something was up if we only schedule five shows."

"Six with the wrap-up episode." Hank paced back and forth. "Seven if we show them going to meet their families."

"Eight if you actually do an episode to memorialize the contestants who died coming here," Margaret said with more than a hint of disgust in her voice for the whole enterprise her brother had made his life's work.

"Ohhh, great idea!" Hank said, completely oblivious to her disdain, deep in hit TV producer mode. "The women who died for a chance at love…" His concentrated acting continued.

"What if they get home and hate each other?" Margaret asked, because really, if she stayed, tomorrow she might wake up and realize she'd made a mistake and then she'd be stuck on Mars with Jack Boyle.

"Even better!" Hank said, a smile spreading across his face.

"That's kind of cruel, Hank," Margaret said, wishing she hadn't eaten the whole second bar.

"Misty won't let that happen. She's a woman on a mission. She wants Chad and she'll keep him," Lynette predicted.

Margaret wondered if it could be that easy. Maybe if the guy was equally as committed. Was Jack committed to her? He wouldn't have offered her this opportunity if he wasn't. She should stay. Live on Mars with Jack.

Maybe she was drunk on sugar and would regret it, but she realized she was going to throw caution to the wind. She was going to do it. She was going to risk everything for love.

"Let's set this up," Hank said, because he was Hank and therefore he would make her insane idea work. "Margo, we can't bring home your rover if we have to fly home the crew members," he said, already turning away, as if that was an afterthought.

"Wait, what?" Margaret said, waking up from her sugar coma.

"We won't have the weight. Maybe Boyle can send it home on his next quarterly shuttle."

They would leave her rover here, which meant she would be screwed at work anyway. How could she work on the finishing pieces of the rover if she had no rover?

Don't grab onto that so quickly, Margaret. You have plenty of things to work on in the lab. If you want Jack, be honest about it.

The man she'd been agonizing over walked in.

"Hank, are you sure about this plan?" Lynette asked, her tone doubtful.

"I'm sure," Hank said. "Let's do this." And out he walked to change the whole game.

Jack stood above her. "Hungry?" he asked, taking in the wrappers and, she realized from his intense study of her face, a chocolate smear on her cheek.

She rubbed at it. "I'm thinking."

"By eating chocolate?"

"That's the best way to do it."

"I just need to tell you one more time…you might be leaving, but we're not done," Jack said again.

That was good. He wasn't giving up and he shouldn't. They were worth a chance. And for once, she was doing exactly what the hell she wanted. She brushed off the wrappers.

Jack offered his hand.

"Thank you," she said as he pulled her to her feet. "You're right, Jack. We aren't done, because I'm staying."

He blinked. "You are?"

"My rover and I don't make the weight requirements for the return shuttle."

"What?"

"Well, I could go without it, but I don't want to. I'm staying to try to see if this thing between us is as wonderful as I think it is."

Jack stood still, as if he struggled with her hundred-eighty degree turn. "You're staying?"

"Yes," she said, never feeling so sure in her life. "And I came up with an idea to get rid of the cast."

Jack grabbed her shoulders. "You did?"

"Yep."

"My God, you're amazing," he said and kissed her.

She leaned into the kiss, twining her arms around his neck. He was worth a risk, the biggest risk of her life. And that scared her, but she wouldn't get everything she ever wanted if she didn't risk it all.

"What's going on here, Boyle?" Hank asked behind them.

She reluctantly pulled her lips from Jack's and discovered her brother watching. He didn't look pleased.

"I'm kissing your sister, Hank," Jack said, grinning at her.

She smiled back. Wow, she was falling for this famous geologist and she was running off to Mars to be with him. She tingled with anticipation and fear. "I'm staying here, Hank," she announced.

"Excuse us for a second, Boyle," Hank said, grabbing her arm and dragging her across the room.

"Hank calm down," she said, trying to pry his fingers off her arm where they were digging into her flesh.

"You're acting very un-Margaret-like here, and I want you to snap out of it."

Jack started to move toward them, but stopped when she shook her head. It was her brother, and she'd deal with him. She pinched Hank's wrist.

"Ouch," he said, jerking his hand back.

She rubbed her arm. "I'm taking a risk, I know, but I would have thought you of all people would celebrate that."

"I take risks, it's true, but you do not, and you need to understand what you're getting into here. Boyle is a major asshole."

"He's not an asshole, Hank. He's too alpha for you to charm or bully, so you don't like him." She loved her brother, but she also understood his failings. "But I like him. We have an amazing amount in common."

Hank stared at Jack as if he spied a mountain lion in the grass. "Like what?"

"We're both scientists, we're both introverts, both driven and focused, both at the top of our fields and focused on the same topic, even if we have different areas of expertise on Mars, and we're sexually compatible."

Her brother's gaze jerked back to hers. "What?"

"You heard me. I may be your sister, but I'm still a woman." She patted her brother's arm, knowing she was freaking him out, but wanting him to understand. "I'm going to stay on Mars and finish my research here—where better to do it? You should know by now that this is the place I've always wanted to be."

"Well, yes, Mars has always been a fixation for you, but Margaret," his gaze turned deeply worried, "I don't want you to get hurt."

Margaret smiled at him, knowing her brother loved her. "I might. I'm taking a big chance that this relationship will work out. But so what if it doesn't? I won't be any worse off than before. I can always go back to Earth and spend my nights alone in a lab somewhere." Of course, she'd have to find a new lab, but she wasn't going to tell Hank that. He'd just use it to argue with her. But the time for arguments was over.

"I don't like this. And neither will Mom and Dad," Hank said, pulling out the big guns.

Margaret blinked at Hank invoking their parents. While she loved them, Margaret hadn't had anything but vague support from them for any goal she'd set. "I know you don't like it. But I let you do all kinds of nutty things without interfering, so I know you'll have the respect for me to do the same." She had a firm policy of only judging her brother quietly inside her own mind.

Hank sighed and shrugged his shoulders. "You're right. I need to let you do this. Hell, it might not even be a mistake."

Margaret snorted. "Gee, thanks." She left the "let you do this" comment alone for now. She could save her feminist lecture for when he was back on Earth.

"Okay, you and your rover are staying. That means I can fit everyone in the return shuttle if we leave all our supplies and equipment here." Hank gave another disgruntled look at Jack. "Boyle said we had to take all our equipment and garbage back off with us. The man is obsessed with trash removal."

"I'm sure he'll understand if you have to leave it all here," she said, making the executive decision that Jack would rather have the people gone and the items here than vice versa.

"I doubt it," Hank said. "But I'll tell him you said so when he throws a fit."

"Go ahead and tell him that." Because Margaret knew to get rid of them, Jack would do almost anything.

CHAPTER SEVENTEEN

Jack stood watching the shuttle take off, filled with all the contestants, crew and poor Walter Haxley, who would be spending some time in a psych ward back on Earth. Jack had never been so relieved in his life.

"I had to make a deal with Hank so all the people could fit weight wise," Margaret told him from where she stood by his side.

"He left all his garbage didn't he?" Jack guessed, giving a small wave in his sheer happiness to be rid of them all.

"Yes."

"How much?"

"Unfortunately all of it."

Jack turned to her. "All?"

"To fit the people, they had to abandon all their equipment and supplies, including the ones the shuttle brought here for the second part of filming."

Jack eyes grew huge. "No," he said, running to his living room. He'd been busy programming the robot to haul their rocket back out to the launch site and hadn't seen the unloading.

When she caught up, she found boxes upon boxes of supplies, dumped among the rows upon rows of camp beds the women had slept on.

"Holy mother of God," Jack whispered, leaning close to read a nearby box, which was labeled SPAGHETTI NOODLES. "It will take us months to eat this."

"On the bright side, you won't have to bring more food here for a long time."

Jack scanned the boxes, seeing crap he'd never use like boxes of makeup and clothes, and things he would, like toilet paper. Lots of it. "You know, if I cancel the quarterly shuttle for next time, I will save a massive amount of money." Enough money to last another six months. And after that, it might be time to go home. The idea held such appeal, he let out a small laugh in celebration.

He grinned, thinking how lucky he was to have found a woman so right for him, who had moved in with months of free supplies.

"We'll need to do an inventory, but you won't need basic supplies again for a long time," she said, leaning over to read another label.

He caught her hand and swung her into his arms. "So, now that we're alone, can I show you our room?"

She rose up on tiptoes to kiss him and he deepened it immediately, all lips and tongue and exploration. Heat poured through him, the need so deep and strong and right. And they were finally, finally alone. He reveled in the feel of the softness of her lips, digging his hands in her hair, pulling out her ponytail and running his fingers through her blond strands.

Somehow, he'd found the perfect partner 140 million miles away from Earth. He wasn't even sure how he'd been this lucky. She was smart, gorgeous, and understood him completely.

When they came up for air, he swept her up into his arms and carried her sideways through the boxes, while she laughed.

"Wait," she said. He stopped and she pointed to a small box sitting on top of another stack. The side read CONDOMS in big letters.

"Why did they need a big box like this? Not that I'm complaining."

"The night before the final rose ceremony, the last three contestants have sexy time with the bachelor."

"That's one hell of a lot of sexy time. And kind of gross."

"It's worked out for us. Let me grab that."

He dipped her down to reach it.

They stumbled without a hint of grace from the living room and into his bedroom, where he tried to gently put her down, but dropped her instead. "My shoulder isn't working like it should," he said, falling onto the bed beside her, careful to land on his good side.

"Poor thing," she said, smiling at him. "We'll have to figure out a place to stack all that."

"Luckily I have space out in the mechanical shed to put things we'll never use." He'd have to pay to haul all Hank's crap back off the planet, but he supposed that was the price for peace and quiet.

"You're assuming Hank didn't put stuff out there too," she said.

"God, your brother," he said, realizing that Hank would not be a distant nightmare if he stayed with Margaret, but rather someone he saw at holidays and family get-togethers.

"I know he's exhausting, but he'll grow on you." She rolled on top of him. "Now that we're alone…"

He switched their positions. "My turn to be on top I think."

"Oh good, I'm ready for someone else to do the work."

They kissed, slow and leisurely, not rushing because they didn't have to. This was the start to a long, enforced cohabitation and they had time to get it right.

She helped him work his shirt off so he didn't hurt his shoulder, spending time after to kiss along the duct tape. "You poor thing," she said, running her tongue along the edge of his bruise.

"Strangely, I can't even feel it right now," he said, stripping off her shirt so he could explore every inch of her perfect breasts.

When they'd touched and kissed every bit of exposed flesh, they both shed their pants, then she rolled on top of him, straddling his hips. "I guess technically I've won the game," she said, in between kisses.

"You didn't end up with Chad."

"No, I ended up with someone better." Someone who matched her on every level. Someone she could grow old talking to about anything and everything under the sun, including Mars.

For a bit she was distracted, arching her hips in rhythm to his, as his large cock slid in her wetness. Then she remembered herself. "Wait a second, cowboy," she said, bracing an arm on his good shoulder, because somehow she was now under him and they were mere inches away from penetration.

He blinked at her as if he were coming out of a sex induced haze, which she figured he was.

"Unless you want to create the first human on Mars..."

"What are you talking about?" he asked.

"Condoms, get a condom," she gasped, hating to break their stride, but really safety first had always been her motto. Of course, she'd forgotten it for a moment there, but it was hard to think, she was so turned on.

"Oh," he said, looking adorably panicked as he picked up the box and wrestled with the packaging, stripping pieces of the tape off and prying off the box top.

Although, when she thought of having a child, instead of her usual caution, for the first time in her life it made her happy. After all, she wasn't getting any younger. She really wouldn't mind having her own little Martian running around the lab. One thing was certain, any child of theirs would be brilliant.

But that thought would have to be saved for a later time, because Jack had a condom finally freed.

"Now we have to start all over again since we lost the mood," he said, but not like he was disappointed more like he was excited to further explore their passion.

"Speak for yourself," she said breathlessly, "but if you need a do over, start here," she said, offering him her breasts to explore, which he did, with the detailed attention of a true scientist.

And just like that, their passion flared to life again. She ran her hands along his muscled abs, the feel of the hardness under the soft skin making her shiver. He had such an amazing body. She wasn't even sure she'd paid attention to how men were put together in the past, but she was pretty sure he was perfect.

When he stopped fumbling with the foil packet, she took the condom from him and spent some time running her mouth over his head, tasting him and enjoying the shiver of need that went through him at her touch.

"Goldie," he growled, obviously growing tired of her teasing, his voice full of need.

She laughed, the sound so full of feminine power, she almost didn't recognize it as her own. But she relented and rolled on the condom.

Then he was inside her, hilting deep, hitting a spot that felt like heaven.

"There," she said.

And with a groan, he repeated the motion, his face a mask of concentration as he attempted to put aside his own need to give her exactly what she wanted.

"Yes," she said, her climax building with an intensity so great it almost frightened her. She'd never felt this way before, even when she'd pleased herself. This was a deep, primal feeling building inside her, one of an impending explosion that she felt might engulf her. And then she was coming, tipping over the edge, taking him with her if his shout of triumph was any indication. Satisfaction and contentment flowed through her body like she had never experienced before. It had been everything she never knew she'd always wanted and more.

They collapsed in a sweaty heap, breathing as if they'd run for hours.

"I'm so glad you decided to stay. Being on Mars just became amazing again," he said, rolling beside her and pulling her close.

"I'm glad you didn't give up when I said no." She draped her body across his and he ran a leisurely hand down her back to brush along her buttocks. She shivered with goosebumps.

He smiled. "I don't ever give up. If I did, I wouldn't have Mars and I wouldn't have you."

THE END

ABOUT THE AUTHOR

*L*eigh Wyndfield lives in rural Virginia with her fat cat Ayra, two lovable rescue puppies, four chickens, and the best guy in the world. A city girl at heart, she's embracing the mysteries of growing things and watching deer race from hunters through her yard. Traveling and driving an ambulance round out her time. She writes romance fiction that is out of this world.

Lightning Source UK Ltd.
Milton Keynes UK
UKHW010738020222
398089UK00001B/86